More to Life
Than Mr. Right

More to Life Than Mr. Right

♦

Stories for Young Feminists
Compiled by
Rosemary Stones

Henry Holt and Company | New York

First published in the United States in 1989 by
Henry Holt and Company, Inc.,
115 West 18th Street, New York, New York 10011.
Published in Canada by Fitzhenry & Whiteside Limited,
195 Allstate Parkway, Markham, Ontario L3R 4T8.
Originally published in Great Britain in two volumes under the titles
More to Life Than Mr. Right, 1985, and
Someday My Prince Will Not Come, 1988, by
Piccadilly Press Ltd., 5 Canfield Road, London NW6 3BT.

Library of Congress Cataloging-in-Publication Data
More to life than Mr. Right : stories for young feminists / compiled
by Rosemary Stones.
     Contents: A family likeness / by Jacqueline Roy — Different rules
/ by Sandra Chick — The sexy airs of summer / by Jean MacGibbon —
Stilettos / by Rosemary Stones — Twelve hours, narrative and perspectives /
by Adèle Geras — India / by Ravi Randhawa — Hermes and Aphrodight / by
Susan Price — The year of the green pudding / by Fay Weldon.
     ISBN 0-8050-1175-7
     1. Short stories, English. [1. Short stories. 2. Feminism—
Fiction.]   I. Stones, Rosemary.
PZ5.M837   1989
[Fic]—dc20   89-11016

First American Edition
Designed by Victoria Hartman
Printed in the United States of America
10 9 8 7 6 5 4 3 2 1

Contents

Introduction

Most young adults would agree that there's more to life than Mr. Right. But as we approach the 1990s, does anybody really need to read "stories for young feminists" anymore?

Maybe not. Maybe we've finally arrived at the stage where feminist issues don't have to be fought for—maybe they can even be taken for granted. Women have made enormous gains since the feminist movement began in the early 1970s. They are working in executive positions. They hold high government posts. They are admitted to private institutions that were at one time exclusively male. They have access to reliable birth control, they can join the armed forces, they cannot legally be discriminated against. Girls are as good as boys, and nobody would say different. What's left for young feminists to read about?

Plenty.

The stories in this collection don't take on directly the major political issues of our time—many of which, arguably, do still need fighting for. They focus instead on subjects that are of much more immediate concern to young women and young men as they come of age in the 1990s. Though these stories are all by British writers, the questions they raise will provoke and excite young adults in this country— just as they excited young adults in the United Kingdom when the stories were published there.

The eight stories are rich and diverse, and were selected to present differing views of and responses to feminism.

Is it permissable—or even possible—for a girl to step into her father's footsteps? "A Family Likeness" explores the idea of whether a daughter can be heir to a tradition that has been exclusively male.

A mother flouts the traditional role in "Twelve Hours—Narrative and Perspectives." It's one thing for a young adult to explore her own sexuality. But should she accept the same behavior from her mom?

"Different Rules" takes on an old problem—that of double standards. But it also bring up other issues: the difficulty of female self-expression in a language that is male-oriented; the self-delusion that can accompany sex without affection.

In "India" and "The Sexy Airs of Summer," affection abounds. The two stories might even be called romances (though one ends happily and the other not). They belong in a feminist collection because they examine the conflict between the romantic ideal and the often less-than-ideal reality. It's a conflict that manifests itself not only in the stories' boy-girl relationships, but in peer pressure and the expectations of family and of society as a whole.

"Stilettos" presents a particularly complex issue: whether feminism is defined by words or action. A similar theme is taken up in "Hermes and Aphrodight." This allegorical story examines traditional ideas about femininity and masculinity, how closely tied they are to appearance, and how much it takes to transcend them.

Finally, Fay Weldon's "The Year of the Green Pudding," a character study, looks at an ordinary woman in an extraordinary situation. Is this the woman of the late twentieth century? Can she be the legacy of the feminist movement?

More to Life Than Mr. Right doesn't preach—nor does it need to. By presenting young adult readers with the kinds of questions and choices they are confronted with every day, it encourages serious thought about growing up female in today's world.

—The Editors

More to Life
Than Mr. Right

A Family Likeness

by Jacqueline Roy

Livy, do you think you'll feel like coming out on Friday?" asked Melanie hesitantly. She'd been building up to asking for at least ten minutes, though she didn't know why she couldn't even ask a simple question anymore. Olivia didn't answer; she merely shook her head without bothering to look up. They continued to walk along the road in uneasy silence.

Melanie was getting tired of trying to get things back to normal. Patience didn't come naturally to her, and she couldn't get used to having to think about every word and action in case Livy was upset by what she said or did. Yet she felt she had to try, because after all they were best friends, and best friends stood by each other for better or for worse. . . . Olivia's whole attitude said very clearly,

Leave me alone, just let me get on with it, and Melanie was often tempted to do just that. And the worst thing was, she was almost relieved that Livy wanted to be by herself so much, despite the efforts she was making to get her out. She wasn't exactly easy to get along with anymore, and she looked so miserable that everybody around her felt miserable too—either that, or guilty because they *weren't* miserable. Sometimes Melanie wondered what it must feel like to have a parent just die on you, as Olivia's father had died on her. But the subject was too big and too awful to be contemplated for any length, and Melanie could only push it to the back of her mind as one of those imponderables, like being put in prison for something you didn't do or living through a nuclear war.

"I wish you would start coming out again," said Melanie, feeling the need to give it one last try. "There isn't any point in moping; he wouldn't have wanted you to. . . ." Melanie faltered here; why did she have to mention Livy's father? She might cry or something, which would be awful. But Olivia's face didn't change, she just continued to plod homeward in the mechanical, uninterested way she'd adopted since the funeral last semester. . . . Melanie suddenly realized it had all been going on for at least three months. How long did the being miserable last? Maybe you never got over it.

Melanie became aware that Livy hadn't even attempted to respond to her question. "Aren't you going to say anything then?" she said crossly, though she wanted to be kind.

"Sorry," said Olivia. "I just don't want to come, that's all."

"Okay, fair enough," said Melanie, but she tried to say it gently.

They fell into silence again. There was a limit to Melanie's ability to converse with someone who didn't want to talk back—or *couldn't* talk back perhaps. Vaguely Melanie sensed there were things that Livy wanted to tell her but couldn't put into words. She'd been so silent since it happened, a silence that at times conveyed an angry hostility but at others held nothing but sadness. Melanie was barely able to deal with either. At fifteen she was beginning to see just how complicated life could be, and the idea of spending the next sixty or seventy years in a state of bewilderment was a daunting prospect. She hoped that age would bring wisdom, but she had her doubts. Her mother, father, and elder sister weren't showing much. Of course, she might manage to be different—wiser, more sensitive, and more aware—

but if her progress with Livy was anything to go by, she was doomed to a life of ignorance. If only Livy would let her do something instead of shutting her out all the time. . . .

They turned off the High Street and walked toward Olivia's gate. Livy began to fumble in her pocket for her keys. "Do you want to come in?" she said.

Melanie looked at her in surprise. Of late, Livy hadn't seemed able to wait to put the front door between them. "Yes, all right," she said, not really relishing the prospect. Her mother had said that Mrs. Everson's grief was such that she was cracking up under the strain. Melanie had never seen anyone cracking up and she wasn't sure she wanted to.

"You don't have to come," said Livy, clearly sensing her reticence.

"No, I'd like to, thanks."

The house hadn't changed; that was something. It was full of nice things, books, plants, pottery, and pictures—sketches mostly, done by Livy's dad. She wondered if it hurt Livy to see them on the walls. It would have hurt her had she been in Livy's shoes. . . .

Perhaps that was the trouble—up until then their lives had been similar; so similar that they'd been drawn to one another since their first day at school. They'd spotted each other across the playground at the age of just five because they looked so much the same; each had short curly hair and golden-colored skin, and later they'd discovered they each had one black parent and one white, that they lived two streets apart, and that they both had a birthday in the last week of August. They'd always felt like twins—until last semester, that is. Melanie was beginning to realize that if Livy's father could die, then hers could too, that nothing was safe or certain. That was why she didn't want to be in Livy's house and why she felt afraid. . . . Why had it been Livy's father and not hers? It could so easily have been her own father who'd died in that accident. ~~Who or what decided things like that? Did it make it better or worse to believe in God?~~

"Would you like something to drink?" said Livy. "There's cola in the fridge."

"They put teeth in a glass of that stuff and they just disintegrated."

"Does that mean no?"

Melanie smiled. "I guess it does. Have you got any fruit juice?"

"Orange or grapefruit?"

"Orange, please."

They sat and looked at each other across the kitchen table, aware that just now, in choosing drinks, they'd almost had a normal conversation.

"Where's your mother?" asked Melanie.

"She'll be back later. She said she'd do some shopping."

"Is she okay?"

"Why shouldn't she be?"

Melanie shrugged. They both knew the answer to that, but perhaps it was better to avoid it.

"Would you like a sandwich?" said Olivia.

Melanie wasn't hungry, but Livy had lost so much weight that you could get two people into her jeans. Maybe if she agreed to have a sandwich, Livy would have one too. "What have you got?"

"Ham, cheese, banana, liver pâté . . ."

"Cheese. I'm thinking of becoming a vegetarian."

"Are you?" said Livy. "I tried it once, but I only managed to keep it up for a few days. Mum got sick of cooking three separate meals, one for her, one for me, and one for Dad. . . . Cheddar or Edam?" she said briskly, drawing the subject away from her father as if she'd moved there inadvertently and had been stung by the memory.

"Edam," said Melanie. "It's less fattening. I've decided I'm going to have a healthy body—do you know how many people die of heart disease each year?" She stopped abruptly. How crass could you get? She just had to talk about dying. It was rather like needing to laugh in church; the more you didn't want to do something like that, the more you just had to do it. She'd be discussing the cost of funerals next.

Livy began to butter some bread. Melanie noted with satisfaction that she was doing two sets. She looked around the kitchen and her eyes rested on the wall opposite. There was a portrait of Livy's father there—a self-portrait, she supposed. Some time before his death, he'd been hailed as the most outstanding black painter and sculptor of his generation. There was a book about him, and he'd been on television.

"Mum put that painting up," said Livy. "I know she thinks of him a lot, but she won't talk about him. I wish she would."

"It's a nice picture," said Melanie. It was an inadequate thing to say, but she couldn't think of anything more. She focused her attention on her sandwich, chewing steadily. Livy had finished hers.

"Would you like to see the others—the other paintings?"

No, I wouldn't like, thought Melanie almost fiercely, but she sensed that an honor was being bestowed on her and that it was important to Livy. It was also the first gesture of friendship to come for some time, so she grasped it quickly. "Yes, all right," she said.

The studio was at the top of the house. They went

upstairs slowly. "I haven't been in here since he died," said Livy, and Melanie couldn't think of an answer.

The room was light and airy—a window spanned one wall. All around were the trappings of an artist: easels, paints, brushes. There was a black-plastic bin full of hardening clay and a powdery dust on the plain wooden floor. As they walked, their footsteps were imprinted on it. Some of the paintings were six feet high. Melanie felt awed by their stature and vibrance. And everywhere, black figures surrounded them, with elongated necks and large heads—heads large enough to house the spirit; Melanie remembered the description from the program.

Olivia wandered around, and Melanie watched her with anxiety; what loss was she feeling now? Yet she seemed more relaxed than she'd been for some time; the room seemed to hold something that eased the pain.

"How do you see yourself?" Olivia asked suddenly.

"How do you mean?"

"Do you see yourself as black or white?"

"I don't know. Neither, I suppose. No, *black*."

Olivia nodded. "Me too. That's why what he did was so important."

Melanie knew what she meant. Part of her own

sense of herself was somewhere in these paintings and sculptures. How much more was it there for his daughter?

"I wish I was like him," said Livy.

"You are like him. Everybody says so."

"Not just to look at. I want to do what he did."

"Paint?"

"Paint and sculpt."

"Why shouldn't you? You're the best in the school at art—even better than the seniors."

"Did you know that his father—my grandfather— was a carver too? And his father before him, and back as far as you can imagine?"

Melanie nodded.

"Then it's up to me to carry on, or the whole thing will be broken."

"Then carry on," said Melanie quietly.

"I'm not his son."

"What does that matter? You're his daughter."

Olivia was crying; Melanie was trying not to look, but she could see it through the corner of her eye. "You're his daughter, Liv. That counts."

"It's always sons."

"He didn't have any sons. Besides, even if he had had them, it would still have been you because you've got the talent—anyone who's seen your paintings would know that."

"But you see, Melanie, I want to do it in order to be part of a tradition, but as a daughter I can't be part of it; I can only break with it."

Melanie felt out of her depth. She sat on a chair without a back by the window. It was covered with spots of dried paint; it looked like a palette. "Did he say you couldn't do it?"

"No. We didn't discuss it. You see, I couldn't ask him to teach me in case he said no, and he never suggested it. I watched him though, and tried to learn that way. He liked me to be here."

"Perhaps he was waiting until you were old enough to be shown properly."

"I wish I knew. I'm not sure whether he would have shown me or not. I want to do it though."

"Then do it, Livy. Go to art school—do whatever you have to do."

"It won't be the way it should be."

"Nothing ever is. Look, things have changed. Even traditions change—they adapt to suit the times. For your father's father, and all those fathers before him, daughters were for cooking and cleaning, just as for the white slave owners blacks were for picking cotton and harvesting bananas or whatever it was. It can all be changed once people realize that it can be. . . . Oh hell, I don't know how to put this, I can't think how to get it across. But I know I'm right. Your father would want you to be a carver and a painter—he'd probably expect it of you. He wouldn't think you were less able or less important just because you're a daughter rather than a son. Livy, just look at his work. It goes beyond men and women; it even goes beyond black and white."

Olivia looked again. As a small child, she'd watched her father chipping and smoothing rough edges, making something live through the large, shapeless slabs. Figures had appeared as if by magic: men and women and children with long necks and large oval heads, masks with angry, scary faces, horses and strange birds from ancient African mythologies. She'd wanted to emulate him, to carve and paint as he did. Her father had shown her each of the figures he'd created, and told her all the stories. She knew about Anansi and Nyankapon, the First Picni and Brer Rabbit. Since his death, she'd gone over all the legends in her mind, preserving them as the only link she now possessed with her past—her history. She had been born of a Jamaican father and an English mother, she was British but she was also black, and she'd been afraid that an important part of that identity had been buried with her father. Now she was coming to realize that it could never be lost, just as the spirit of her father could never be lost either; it lived on in the work he'd left behind him, and it lived on in her.

Olivia walked around, remembering all her father had taught her, how each piece of wood, each stone, held an image waiting to be freed; how the carver simply let it out. She touched each one of the shapes she saw, felt its roughness or its smoothness in her fingertips. She too could free the animals and birds and children trapped in their inanimate materials. And all around the walls, figures looked down at her in paint, in wood, in stone; timeless forms, the spirits of her past brought to life. She saw and felt their colors and was soothed.

She was her father's daughter; she had the right to inherit his skills.

Different Rules

by Sandra Chick

I t's a bit of a mess in here," he said.

"Don't worry about it," I said.

"Not *worried*," he said, "just saying."

He unlocked the door, put his hand inside, and switched the light on. I followed him into the room.

"This isn't a *mess*," I said, "more like a war zone."

"Well I reckon it's *friendly*," he said. "It's got character. D'you want tea or coffee or something?"

"What 'something' have you got?" I said.

"Well," he said, "I've got tea, coffee, tea, or coffee."

"In that case I'll have tea."

I unzipped my coat and took it off, threw it over the chair, on top of his jacket.

It's funny when you see somebody else's place for

the first time; it's never how you imagined it. There were empty bottles and cans, part of a bike, heaps of clothes.

We squeezed past the sofa—a huge blue nylony thing that you had to fight with to get to the kitchen. When I say *kitchen,* I mean a sink, two cabinets, and a table abandoned in one corner.

"What d'you think of the color scheme then?" he said.

"Um . . . it's not exactly subtle," I said. "Sort of . . ."

"Jumps out to get you," he said.

"Yeah, you could say that," I said.

There were greens and yellows in flowery patterns.

"Clashes nicely though."

"Keep meaning to do it up," he said. "Not into this decorating stuff though. Don't s'pose you picture yourself with a paintbrush?"

"No," I said. "I don't."

"Didn't think so," he said, starting to organize mugs, tea bags, and kettle.

I pointed at the muddy Styrofoam dish on the draining board.

"What was that?"

"Chow mein," he said, "from the new place. It was good at the time—honest."

"Dare I ask when that was?" I said.

"Yesterday, no, day before."

"I'll take your word for it," I said, "but it looks like a museum exhibit to me."

He handed me a carton of milk.

"Taste that, see what it's like."

"You do it," I said.

"I hate sour milk," he said. "Oh, all right, give it here then."

He sniffed it.

"I'd recommend it *without*," he said, and poured it down the drain, semisolid. The smell was sharp and sickly.

"You're disgusting and it'll clog," I said.

"I'm not and it won't," he said. "Not if I run the hot water, blast it away."

He dropped the leftover takeout into the trash can; the flap didn't open and so he kicked it. Then he picked up a cloth and wiped the table over. It was dull and covered with heat rings.

"Look at that," he said, winking. "Good as new."

"At least," I said.

We'd always got along well—in our own way. Messed around, had a laugh, usually at other people—the rest of the crowd—they were so *serious* sometimes. We'd do our double act, giving them a hard time until they gave in. Or until they'd had enough of us and got up and left.

I felt disappointed if he wasn't around. Wondered what he was doing, who he was with. He'd said a couple of times that I ought to come around—if I had nothing else to do. I didn't say no. I was waiting, hoping he'd say a particular night; then I'd know he really meant it.

I always thought something'd happen between us eventually. But it's difficult to ask someone out. I thought maybe he was scared I'd turn him down, make him feel stupid. Still, now I was here. I felt pretty good.

He handed me the tea, then introduced me to his two dead plants, Daphne and Delilah, and his pet stone.

"Don't touch it," he said. "It's so vicious—it'll take your arm off."

"Never mind that," I said. "I just hope you sterilized this mug. Or does it carry a health warning?"

"Come on," he said, "don't give me a hard time—or I'll shut you in the trunk, out of the way."

"Ah, I noticed that thing," I said.

"That *thing*," he said. "Charming. That *thing*'s an antique, y'know."

It stood to one side, old and weighty. The wood was scratched, but somehow it managed to look good.

"What's in it?" I said.

"Only a few bits and pieces. And the body of the last person that hassled me," he said.

I lifted the lid. Turned over a couple of paperbacks that lay on top of the magazines and junk.

"Damn it. She must have escaped again," he said, raising his eyebrows and putting on his innocent expression—the one he always uses when he's talking trash. He was leaning against the wall, hands by his side, tapping his fingers against a patch of bare plaster. That's something else he does—taps his fingers, same old beat, one two three, one two three. Drives people crazy; the more they complain, the more he does it to wind them up.

"Anyway, stop being nosy," he said. "Come and sit down."

There was no space on the sofa; it was taken up with records and a defunct stereo system. We sat on the bed.

"One day," he said, "I'm gonna land myself a great apartment with all the stuff in it—carpets up to my ankles, twin Jacuzzi, robot to clean up . . ."

"That all?" I said.

"Well," he said, "I'd settle for anything that had two rooms—and a bathroom I didn't have to share with ten others. Be fine. But even that's out of reach."

"We could rob a bank," I said.

"Or marry millionaires," he said. "On second

thought, no. Fed up with being judged on how much cash is in my pocket."

"Don't want to get married, either," I said.

He smiled.

"You're not *aching* for a frilly dress and a string of bridesmaids then?"

I laughed.

"Well, of course, to tell the truth, I'm obviously en route to marriage via the shortest possible road— I mean, I've gotta be, don't I?"

"Now, now," he said, "we'll have less of the sarcasm. I know what you mean, though."

"People seem to think there's something wrong with you if you don't want what they've settled for," I said.

"They want to know why, you mean—like there must be 'some reason.' "

"And what if there is 'some reason'?" I said.

"Ah, but you forget, they're ignorant."

"Ignorance is no excuse," I said. "Makes me sick."

"My old man says I'll 'come around' to getting hitched," he said.

"Well, I'm not saying I'll be on my own till the day I die," I said. "I'm saying I'll do what I want, when I want."

"Why not?" he said. "Do what you like. Who cares what anybody else thinks? I don't."

He paused, gulped his tea. I wasn't drinking mine. It was strong, I take it weak.

"Remember that time we all took off down the coast?" he said.

"Yeah, yeah," I said, "and my mother reported me missing to the police."

He laughed.

"That's right, yeah. You had no business being out that late, young lady."

"But what about when a certain person dived into the sea and cut his legs to pieces?"

"Don't change the subject," he said.

"Well, all I can say is, thank God they never actually found me till I was home again," I said. "Would've been the embarrassment of all time."

"Wouldn't have locked you up or anything," he said. "Not in a cell—maybe a playpen, but not a cell."

"Ha, ha," I said.

"Good laugh, though," he said. "Nobody seems to do anything anymore."

"We should," I said. "Soon. Let's do something, say, next weekend?"

"Have to see," he said, shrugging.

"Or let's do something *now*."

"Such as?"

"I don't know."

"Bit limited I'm afraid, dear," he said, "unless you planned on terrorizing the neighborhood or something, painting a few obscene slogans around town."

"Stupid," I said. "Where were you going tonight, anyway? Don't usually see you just wandering around the streets."

"Just wandering," he said, "sums it up."

"Bar out of favor now?"

"I went in for one," he said. "Same old thing. Lenny telling me how I should've been there last night, had a great time, got smashed, had his head down the john all night."

"Great time," I said.

"Lost his license this week," he said. "Definitely won't see him sober for the next year now."

"Anybody else around?"

"Not really," he said. "Just Lenny and that, what's she called—girl with the long hair, you know?"

"Kim?" I said.

"That's it. Think she's gone back home with him."

"Rather her than me," I said.

"Let's phone him up," he said, "get him going."

"You've got a *phone?*" I said.

"Actually, that's why I said it. Knew you'd be impressed."

"We shouldn't *really,*" I said.

"Come on," he said. "For a laugh."

It was on the floor with everything else. He lifted the receiver. Got a wrong number.

"Dunno who that was," he said, tried again, got it right. As soon as there was an answer from Lenny, he hung up. Did it four or five times, trying not to give himself away.

"He'll be freaking out," he said.

"He'll get you back," I said.

"How's he gonna know it's me," he said, "if he couldn't even spot a cop car tailing him for two miles?"

It amused him, and, for some reason, me.

We talked about how Lenny'd been caught, hauled in, drunken drivers in general. Then football rowdies and muggers. Still left time for the last film we'd seen, the best and worst ads on TV, who was working where, and who wasn't working at all.

He leaned over and pulled two cans of beer from under the bed, separated them.

"Forgot I had these left," he said. "Definitely un-chilled, but good enough."

"Tea and lager," I said.

"I know," he said. "I'm so sophisticated."

He shook his can, pointed it at me, and pulled the ring. I ducked, and the bitter foam sprayed a pile of clean T-shirts.

"Shit," he said. "Didn't know you could move that fast."

"It'll give you something to do tomorrow," I said.

"Umm," he said, and paused. "I lie here till lunch-time sometimes, trying to think of something to do."

"Slob," I said.

"*I am not.*"

"Thought you said you don't care what anyone thinks?"

"Yeah, well, I don't. . . . All right, I get your point."

"What d'you do all day, really?" I said.

"I sit here," he said, "waiting for something to happen, only it never does."

He put his head in his hands and pretended to cry.

"Fool," I said.

"Okay then, what about you?" he said.

"I make lists."

"Like?"

"Like do washing, see if the mail's arrived, buy newspaper."

He laughed.

"There's me cooped up here, waiting for my life to start, and you writing never-ending lists about nothing—p'raps we're both crazy."

He put his fingers up to his face, making them into claws, hissed.

"Not funny though, is it?" he said.

"Maybe something'll turn up," I said. "Workwise, I mean."

"Maybe," he said. "Till then I'm on the outside looking in."

We didn't speak for a while. He lay still, head buried in the down comforter. It was past midnight, and quiet.

I glanced up at some photos pinned to the wall, stretched to get a better view. They were old, but I recognized a few faces that were still around.

Looked at the room again properly. He was right, I thought, about the chaos—it added something rather than took anything away. Without the clutter it'd just be a square, a cube, a box.

There were books that I couldn't imagine him reading. Music I couldn't imagine him playing.

It was shabby, but a bit like a kid's room in ways. A cloth parrot on a perch, an inflatable snake dangling from the ceiling.

He lifted himself onto his elbows and reached for his drink.

"Still breathing, then?" I said.

He sat up, swiveled around.

"Okay—how many times d'you reckon your average person breathes in, say, a year?" he said.

"Is this a joke?" I said.

"No. Come on. How many?"

"How should I know?"

"Work it out—minute, hour, day, year."

"Shut up," I said.

"I know," he said.

"How many then?"

"It's obviously . . . *a lot.*"

I grabbed the pillow, threw it at him. He caught it.

"Missed," he said, looking at me, grinning. Kept looking, kept grinning.

"What you looking at?" I said.

"Seeing how many times you blink in a minute."

"You're so *mature* sometimes," I said.

"There you go again," he said. "Real sarcastic."

"So?" I said.

"Well, I was only *looking.*" He said, "D'you know you've got funny eyes?"

"And what d'you mean by *funny?*" I said, covering them.

"Well, sort of *funny.* Screwed up. Come here," he said. "Let me see."

He put his hand under my chin to turn my head up to the light. The bulb was bright and bare.

"Get off," I said. "What d'you expect under that thing? It's like something from a spy movie."

"You've finally figured me out," he said. "I'm a secret agent. But if it's bothering you . . ."

He pulled the cord and the light went out.

"That better?" he said.

"Well, at least I can't see *you*," I said.

Just then the telephone rang.

"That bastard Lenny," he said, and let it ring.

Telling you, I feel like I should start defending myself here. Sounds like some gag—"What d'you do when you run out of conversation?" But it was my decision and I felt okay with it, nothing to do with anyone else.

At the same time, it was weird, though. I had all these crazy thoughts going through my mind. Like, What if the door bursts open and someone barges straight in, sees us? Or, What if the house is burning down and I have to run out into the street, naked? He kept saying, "Relax."

And I kept thinking, What if . . . ?

The sound of voices and traffic gradually got louder. I asked him if he was awake; he said he wasn't. The bed was pushed up against the window. I leaned over, pulled the curtain back, looked out the window. Daylight flooded in. He grunted in disapproval, covered his head with the sheet.

A woman in the room opposite was trying to get her son ready for school. He wouldn't stand still or straight, she slapped him, and he began to cry. The shop below them had opened its doors; a girl carried a board out to the front—CIGS/MILK/COLD DRINKS/SANDWICHES. Workers dashed in and out; a few kids milled around. Occasionally someone would glance up, their eyes focusing on me for a split second.

"You going or staying?" he said. "Only, whatever you're doing, put that bloody curtain back."

"I wonder where they're all going?" I said.

"Who?" he said.

"Them, out there."

"Who cares?" he said.

I dropped the curtain.

"Just a thought."

It was difficult to rest. Each time I moved, he tutted.

A quarrel started in the next apartment.

"I've had enough of this!" she shouted.

"And what d'you expect *me* to do about it?"

"Anything. But do *something."*

I asked him who they were.

"People," he said.

"D'you know them?" I said.

"Not really. They're just people. Ignore it."

"They always like this?"

"Why don't you go and ask them," he said, sighing.

I was uncomfortable. A door slammed; footsteps rained down the stairs.

I crawled out from under the covers, out of the sticky warmth into the cold. Began to dress. My shirt was crumpled on the ground. I pulled my jeans on; one sock was still in the leg, the other was missing.

"What time is it?" he said.

"Quarter past eight."

"What?" he said. "Can't be, not already."

He got up slowly, stretched, gathered his clothes together.

"You off somewhere?" I said.

"Eight thirty," he said. "Moving my sister into yet another dump."

He started dressing alongside me.

"Still, with any luck I won't have to put up with it for much longer," he said.

"Getting out?"

"Right out. May as well. Nothing here."

"S'pose not. Anywhere in mind?"

"Yeah. Well, not definite. But there must be loads of places better than here."

"When's this happening then?" I said.

"Not sure yet. Soon," he said.

He looked at the poster that'd fallen down from the wall.

"Rotten thing," he said. "It's the damp."

The corners had torn. He tried to restick it with the same pieces of tape, pressed his thumbs hard against it.

"What's the point?" he said, letting it drop again.

A horn blared outside.

"Shit—that'll be Chris," he said, "with the van."

He went to the window, put his hand up, and mouthed, "Five minutes." Then opened it and shouted, "I said—five minutes."

I stood in front of the mirror, brushing my hair. Looked a state. "Rats' tails," "Burned string," my mother used to say. Wasn't far wrong.

He laced his boots, searched for money, keys.

"Look, I gotta go," he said. "Lock the door and that. I'll probably see you around, okay?"

"Probably," I said.

I put the brush down. Went over to the window, felt the breeze. Watched them in the street.

Chris had been on his way in; they'd met and were laughing.

"Average," he was saying.

"What's average?" Chris said.

"Well, I mean she wasn't bad," he said. "Passable."

" 'Member our shag-a-slag nights?" Chris said, and they laughed some more before driving off.

There's no word for a male "slag," is there? Only congratulations. Funny, that. Not that it makes me laugh.

The Sexy Airs of Summer

by Jean MacGibbon

D on't have sex with a boy, not for the first time, unless you like him quite a lot," my mother said, "because he probably won't be very good at it. But if you're fond of him, you won't mind."

She was on her knees as she spoke, pinning up the lining of my miniskirt so that it didn't show. "I'll have to rehem this," she said. "Do stand still."

"Don't see that being fond of a boy's got much to do with it, not necessarily," I replied, turning around to see my back view in the long mirror. My new, bright-pink leather miniskirt that I'd bought in the Chapel Street market was just right for the hot weather we were having. To go with the skirt, I'd chosen a white cotton vest top with a wide neck, white lacy tights, and black patent-leather sling backs.

I could be older than sixteen, I thought, looking at the highlights in my brown hair. I'd just had it permed—a "shaggy" perm.

"Oh, but it does, Tracy." She sat back on her heels. "It does matter. I don't mean you can't have a good time without caring for the man, but I'd hate to think of you your first time . . ."

"It's okay, Mum. You don't have to worry. Look, this skirt. It needs the button moved. Could be tighter."

Truth is, Mum's as soppy as they come, a real romantic. But she works for the city council; her boss has to do with family planning or something. So she comes out with these crude remarks, while underneath she's not so sure as she sounds. I got the feeling that she'd like to see me bedded down with a nice steady boyfriend as soon as I was old enough—and she didn't know any more than me when that would be. At the same time she imagined me floating out of a mist toward my beloved like a TV commercial for shampoo.

It's true she didn't have to worry. I was still a virgin. What's more, I bet it was the same for lots of us in my class—not only the girls either, in spite of all the talk. But it bothered me a bit; I wondered sometimes if I was frigid.

School was *so* boring. Most of us were staying on because there were no jobs and you might as well be doing something. A few had left and were living on social security, like Lee Masters, the most gorgeous boy in our year. Like all the girls, I liked him—from a distance. He could get any girl he wanted, but his wants didn't include me.

The only boy I knew who had definite plans was Garry Beale. He was a year ahead of me at school, but we lived in the same street and often walked home together. He was set on studying engineering, going abroad—to Africa. Another time it was South America. He talked a lot—never stopped. But he was interesting, not the usual chatting-up. In a sort of way we got to know quite a lot about one another just through walking home, though not much about personal things. I mean, I knew he had a girlfriend, but he never spoke about her. He was politically minded, which I'm not, and she was too. They were both in Citizens for Nuclear Disarmament and went to demonstrations—not my scene at all. Her name was Anita, a friend told me. He never asked me out, and I never expected him to, what with his having so much on his mind, and being older.

"You're all right, Tracy, nice to talk to, know what

I mean?" he'd say. If I'd had a brother, I sometimes thought, he could have been a bit like Garry.

Or so I thought till the night we met on my way to the Youth Club. I was wearing the new outfit that I'd bought in Chapel Street. Hot weather turns me on. A dusty, gusty wind blowing up my tights sent shivery, shimmery feelings all over my skin. Words came into my head: "The sexy airs of summer"— something like that. Out of a school poetry book most likely.

In the street where the Youth Club was, Garry came running down the steps of a house, a bundle of leaflets under one arm, his free hand brushing his red-brown hair off his forehead.

He stopped when he saw me.

Dancing had begun at the club, the sound of the beat hitting the house fronts and bouncing back.

"Coming in?" I suggested. Not that he ever did, but I quite wanted him to. He didn't answer, just stood looking at me.

"Anything wrong?" I asked, put out.

"Nah . . . it's just—you look different somehow."

"About time," I said. "I feel a bit different. Coming in, then?"

"Sorry. I've got these to deliver. And there's a meeting."

It's the pink skirt or something, I thought. He

doesn't like it. I passed by, surprised at my irritation. Till that moment I'd never cared what Garry thought of me.

The first boy I saw in the club was Lee Masters, dancing with a girl with blond spiky hair. His brightly patterned shirt was open to the waist, showing an even suntan.

When Lee saw me, he dropped his partner's hand and came over.

"Hi, gorgeous—where ya bin all my life?"

Which was insulting, not to say corny, as we'd gone through school together, though without exchanging a single word that I remember. I said as much. He only grinned. "Never the way you look tonight, sweetheart!"

After that we danced, our hands slippery, our whole bodies bathed in sweat, till we were almost the only couple left on the floor. It was a heady feeling being picked by Lee in front of all the other girls, confirming my new feelings about myself, exciting, uncertain as they were.

"Let's get out of here!" he said.

Outside he took my wrist and led me down the street, which was L-shaped, ending in a railway bridge, and through that to a canal.

I don't know what I expected. I was ready to be kissed. But I was unprepared for what happened under the bridge. He twisted me around, hurting my arm, and shoved me up against the brickwork. With his body pressed against mine, his free hand fumbling up my skirt to get at my tights, he covered my mouth with his mouth, wet, slobbery, suffocating. Struggling, I turned my head sideways and hit him on the face. I was wearing a ring, which scored his cheek.

"You little bitch!" Still gripping my arm, he put up his free hand and saw the blood off his cheek. "Rotten little cow! Bin asking for it all evening, haven't you. *Haven't you?*"

I broke free, stumbled, broke the strap on one of my slingbacks, ran till I reached the corner of my own street.

And ran straight into Garry. He put out his arms and held me. I had my face on his chest, sobbing with breathlessness. He stroked my head and neck, and gently put my wet hair behind my ears. Didn't ask what had happened, just went on stroking me. I felt his heart hammering against my cheek.

Gradually my trembling stopped. I put my face up and he kissed me. We kissed, and held each other, and all the feelings I'd had that night ran into one strong feeling and flowed into him. It was as though we were one person.

"Oh, Tracy!" he whispered. I'd never looked at him properly before. His brown eyes had goldy tints in them and his eyelashes were the same color as his red-brown hair. We sat down on the steps of someone's house. We walked slowly home with our arms around each other, stopping sometimes for a long kiss.

We couldn't meet the next day, Sunday, because I'd promised to go with my parents to spend the day with Gran. All the following week we walked back from school, holding hands and stopping now and then for a kiss. But it was never quite the same as that first time when we were taken by surprise. Our kisses were hurried, and there were always people around. He wasn't crazy about staying out too long, with his exams coming up. "It all depends on how well I do," he said when I complained. "Everything depends on my results—whether I can go to college."

I was supposed to be working for exams as well—not that I expected to pass in more than two, English, perhaps, and home economics. Oh, and I was quite good at art. Only, unlike Garry, I couldn't concentrate: I thought about him all the time.

My first big disappointment came when he was away for a whole week, on a study course, he said.

"What about Anita?" I asked suspiciously when he told me.

"We split up" was all he said. And I believed him. He showed no surprise at my knowing about Anita, and he didn't want to talk about her now. Garry only spoke about what was on his mind at the moment. Maybe this is one difference between boys and girls. Girls tell each other more about their feelings; they discuss each other.

This easy, intimate talk was something I was going to miss with Garry. But at the time I only wanted one thing. And I knew that he did.

The evening after he came back we went down by the canal. We sat down near a clump of willows, and Garry put his arm around me and I put my head on his chest. I told him about Lee Masters under the railway bridge. "He said I was 'asking for it.'" I looked up, expecting to see him ready to murder Lee.

To my surprise he only said, "Lee's a real little chauvinist pig. But, Tracy," he went on, "you *were* looking sexy. No doubt about it. That's fine, but you've got to watch out for shits like Lee."

"You thought that when we met—when you had the leaflets?"

"I'll say! I'd never seen you look like that before."

This really did surprise me. "I thought you didn't like my new clothes or something."

He laughed and held me tighter. "It had nothing to do with the clothes you were wearing, sweetie! It was the way you looked."

"How long have you known—I mean, have you felt like that about me before?"

"Quite a time. What about you?"

I thought back. "I suppose I must have. But I didn't know. It was easy being with you—safe. Different from anyone else. But I never . . . Why didn't you show what you felt?"

"Didn't want to spoil things. You seemed so much younger than me." He gave me a quick kiss. "Till that night. Besides, you went around with your own friends. I never thought you'd . . ."

"Like you? Well, I do now," I said.

I clasped my fingers around his neck and pulled his face down to mine. We rolled sideways, holding each other closely. Then he pushed me away and sat up. People were passing along the towpath.

"If only we could be alone for a bit. Really alone."

But there wasn't anywhere, not even a park, unless you count an open space with paths and seats and geraniums, and a keeper in a little hut to keep an eye on anything that might be going on. And our own homes were no good, with the living room and the TV and everyone sitting around.

As the weeks went by, I grew more and more tense and dissatisfied. What I'd not foreseen was that he would carry on his life more or less as before. He even took the odd Saturday off playing basketball for the school!

There were things I could do, of course. The Youth Club. Going down to the market with my friends. Once or twice we went ice-skating at the Sports Center, but my mind wasn't on it, and people complained that I wasn't fun to be with anymore.

"I think about you all the time," I said one evening. We had turned into an old graveyard with sooty gravestones and high office blocks all around. "I think about you all the time. At school, at night. I don't believe you think about me hardly ever."

"You know I do. I've thought about you for—well, a year, anyhow. Longer than you have. You're a part of my life."

"Only a part?"

"You know what I mean, Tracy. What are we arguing about anyhow? What's bothering you?"

"It's all too—oh, don't you see?" I cried. "If we carry on like this, it'll all get stale and boring. Remember what it felt like the first time you kissed me? We've been to supper with each other's families, everyone's pleased, and they smile and think we're a couple of school kids."

He caught my arm. "What *do* you want? I don't believe you know, not for certain."

"You know quite well what I want."

At that he took me in his arms and kissed me roughly. I could feel his body hard against mine. "I want it too. I want it so much that . . ." He drew away. "It might spoil what we've got. It scares me when I think about what we might lose."

I guessed he was thinking about the future, the years before we could be together properly. This may sound too serious. But Garry *was* serious. I'd had to face this—he thought too much about his future, about whether he'd get a job. That sort of stuff. But it didn't keep him from being sexy. I could feel that. I wanted him so much, the rest didn't seem important.

"Don't think of anything except us, here and now," I said. "Come to my place. Mum and Dad are away for the night next Wednesday. We'd be together for a whole evening, just like we've always wanted."

On Wednesday I prepared a cold supper, did my hair, and waited. One of Mum's sensible ideas had been to tell me where I could get fixed up with the Pill when I needed it. ("I'll give you a doctor's name. But do go in good time." I called the doctor about a month ago. She did fix me up.)

My fear was that Garry might not come. No reason—but when you want someone terribly, you have that fear. I was all set to sit down and take things easy—have a beer, perhaps. There were cans in the fridge. But when he came, we fell into one another's arms in the hall, stumbled into the living room and onto the couch. He kissed my neck and shoulders and began to pull my vest top over my head, trembling so that I had to help him.

The couch was too small.

I said we should go up to my room. I'd taken the bed cover off already. I'd even spread a clean bath towel over the sheet! In theory I knew what happened when two people made love. But by the time I had undressed and lay on the bed, legs apart, my eyes tight shut, I didn't feel anything. The deep unending ache had gone.

He sat on the bed. I waited. After a bit I opened my eyes. He was sitting there with his head in his hands. He hadn't taken his clothes off.

"What's the matter?"

"It's no good. Not like this. I'm sorry."

I knelt up and wanted him to lie down beside me and we could be quiet together, but he shook his head miserably. He couldn't look at me.

"Is it my fault?"

"No. Well . . ." And now he did look up, with a ghost of a smile, glancing at the bed. "It *is* a bit clinical somehow!" (Later we were able to laugh at that first time. The way I was lying spread out, I might have been all set for an operation! It was enough to turn anyone off. But at the time it was bad for us both. Worse for him.)

"I'd better go. Don't be mad at me, Tracy."

"I'm not."

"Just so long as you haven't given up on me."

At the door he said, "It would have been easier outside, I think. But—"

I panicked, sensing that if he walked out now, with that deep, proud shame, it might finish things between us. "I'd like that," I said, trying to play it cool. "How about next Sunday? We could take a bus. Real country—I'd like that."

"Would you?"

"And, Garry—let's not think anymore about tonight. It's not important. You can't *plan* too much to make love, not when we feel the way we do. At least that's what I think. . . ." I trailed away uncertainly.

"Tracy, love." He looked at me at last. "Sunday, then."

He called for me about eleven. He knew where to go. We took a city bus to the terminus. Then a country bus, past cottages, villages, wide skies, and sweeping, gently hilly fields.

We got out at a bar called The Green Man and

went into the cool garden. There was a little river, with ducks looking for crumbs. Garry brought out a Coke and a cider, some cheese rolls and potato chips. I asked him about the ducks, and felt easier once we'd begun talking. He knew what they were called—the different kinds.

"Those are mallards, the ones with the beautiful greeny-blue necks. They're drakes. The females are those browny ones with a purple flash on their wing feathers."

It was quite nice being with a boy who could tell you things.

When the bar closed, we walked along by the river, holding hands. In the afternoon heat everything was still except the water rippling over the stones. Too still. I felt nervous and tense, and our hands were sweaty. Beside a deep pool we sat down and cooled our feet in the water. We kissed and were careful and gentle with each other. We kept looking down the path. No one came, but it was a public footway.

At last he said, "Let's go on."

We climbed a stile into a lane full of sunlight, curving uphill. We walked on with our arms about each other, the long dried grasses tickling our bare feet. A feeling was building up inside me, a long wave that mustn't break too soon. He held me tightly. Weak with love, I couldn't have gone on walking unsupported. It was as though we were waiting for something, somewhere.

Around the bend we came to the place. A great field of clover, red as raspberry juice. To one side tall, dark trees shielded us from the sun.

A dove was cooing.

"Did you know," Garry began, "they fight like anything, doves?"

I put up a hand to stop his mouth.

We walked into the field, and when we lay down, the deep clover came up all around us.

This time we both knew it was going to be all right.

Stilettos

by Rosemary Stones

I'd seen the notice for Saturday work in Ridley's window and called up. When I got there, the manageress was by the register talking to some other girl. She was being interviewed for the same job before me, and she would have got it except that the manageress decided that I was better looking. Turns out the manageress's name is Lynette and she's a real bitch.

I don't mean I'm not glad she thought I was nice looking. I know I'm not bad, if I'm being honest, although you can't say it about yourself. I've got blue eyes and long brown hair, and I don't get zits. My boobs are a bit small for my liking (can't think why, my mum and my gran have got enormous ones, and I thought it was supposed to run in families), and my butt is a bit big. But the point is, I don't think people should get jobs because of what they look like. I felt bad when Lynette said she chose me because nice-looking girls are what the customers like. It's only a shoe shop, after all.

Lynette's nice looking of course—very black clear skin, small and sort of delicate but with a good figure. She only takes size-three shoes.

She doesn't behave like a manageress. She's twenty-four, right, and she gets to say what happens in her shop even if she does have to check with the main office. I think that's really good. But you should see her with guys. When there's a halfway decent man around, she starts flirting and simpering and making really crude jokes. She'll even do it with the policemen from Endell Street station when they walk past. And what she wears underneath!

Once when the shop was quiet, she left Zoë in charge and me and her went to TopStyle around the corner because she'd heard they'd got some new things in. You should have seen Lynette in the changing room. I wear bikini briefs, but if you blinked you'd miss hers. They were just a tiny triangle at the front and a bit of string holding it on. I've seen them kind on sale in shops, but I never thought anyone wore them. You could see all her butt. I didn't know where to look, but Lynette's going: "Here, Nicki, try this on! How d'you think I look in this?" so I suppose that's what she wears every day. It can't be exactly comfortable, but then again I suppose it turns her boyfriend on. I bet they have a whale of a time when they get home.

Lynette turns out to be a moody cow and all. When she gets in a mood, the rest of us can't do nothing right. Even when there's no customers, she's screaming at us to stop chatting and get going. Get going with what? Once she has me lugging a whole consignment of men's shoes up two flights to the stockroom on my own because she has it in for me that day. I was knocked out afterward. I don't think that kind of thing's funny, although she obviously did: "Cheer up then, Nicki! There's another twenty cartons coming in next Saturday."

The thing that gets me most is the way she gets sarcastic when me and the other girls talk about anything other than clothes and men: "Setting the world to rights again, girls! Regular little brain boxes, you are, but you don't know nothing about life."

Our shop's just off Mere Street market, and there's always some group or other at the end of the market selling their newspapers or handing out leaflets. Sometimes they'll have a placard. It's these two women in clodhoppers quite often selling *Militant* and sometimes this black couple from Anti-Apartheid with their kids, telling you not to buy things from South Africa. I go along with them. I never buy Cape oranges and grapes. It's hard though, down at the market, because a lot of the stuff's not labeled and they think you're nuts when you ask where it's from. Sometimes it's the National Front. They look like normal guys. They don't so much say things to black people going past as look them over and crowd them off the pavement. I've even seen them do it to a black woman on her own with a stroller and small kids.

One Saturday they're standing there at the usual spot at the end of the market, which is almost outside our shop, when Lynette sees these two policemen walking by and decides to have a laugh. "Officer!" she goes in a real loud voice. "Could you move these people away from my shop? I don't want odd shoes at the end of the day."

"Ain't us that's the thieves around here, love," goes one of them. The police make them move to the opposite corner, where we can't see them from the shop. Lynette thinks it's really funny, but the fact is she's chancing it. People like that, they can always come back and get you some other time when there won't be two policemen around.

She is good at her job though. She's got a nose for bogus credit cards. Sometimes it's obvious, like when this man had a card with the name Hilary Pulford on it. We all just laughed at him. Afterward someone told me that you can have men called Hilary—not a Mere Street market roughneck though, somehow. Another time this girl had glued a strip of paper over the name on the card. You can tell by the way they do the signature, as well. If they take ages and they're thinking about it, it's stolen. Half of them have a check already signed. Lynette takes the card into the back to call up, and most of them leave when she does that. One girl begged and begged to have the card back. She was really pale and ill looking. Most likely a druggie, Lynette said. Lynette always says if there's real trouble, they can have it—shoes, cards, money. "I'm not getting hurt for the sake of Mr. Ridley and his shoes. He won't thank me." Not that she exactly stuck to that when we did have trouble.

It was coming up to my GCSEs. My mum made me promise not to work the weekend before the exams, but Lynette phones up to say that Zoë's off sick and can I come to help out. My mum couldn't very well say no to her when Lynette had let her have a staff discount on shoes for herself and for my dad. She's the sort who reminds you.

It's one of those frantic Saturdays and I must have run up to that stockroom about one hundred and fifty times. Lots of stupid people who didn't know their own shoe size and all. Kensington branch rings up to ask if we've got any Nina size five left, but I'm so rushed off my feet I just say no without even looking. They sound like a real load of snobs, the girls from that Ridley's branch.

I sometimes go into other branches of Ridley's out of curiosity. It's funny to see it all from the outside as a customer.

Anyway, at closing time Lee (she's the other Saturday girl) and me are doing the shutters and locking up the front while Lynette's cashing up in the back. Then we hear a kind of scuffling noise. We go in and Lynette's standing there, very quiet for her, with two white guys, one young looking and skinny with a leather jacket, and one older and fat. Then I see the fat one's holding a bit of lead pipe. Lee starts up: "Excuse me, we're closed!" before she sees what's what and shut up. Then we all just stand there.

"We'll have the key to the safe and a few pairs of shoes and all while we're here, darlings," goes the fat one with the lead pipe in his hand. "You two little tarts can get the shoes sorted while this one," he's looking at Lynette, "can find us that key."

I'm watching Lynette while he's talking. Her eyes are signaling. That's what makes me pull myself together and start thinking—the fact that Lynette's the one most likely to get hurt, yet she's signaling to me and Lee to stay cool. Lee and me don't say nothing. We start piling boxes of shoes into trash-can-liner bags. Then the skinny one goes: "Not very sexy, these shoes, girls! Ain't you got nothing but old granny shoes?"

"There's this one," says Lee. She's really shaking, but she won't let him see it. She gets a pair of Satin.

Personally I think Satin is a nasty shoe. It's a black-satin stiletto with a six-inch heel like a dagger and at the back a crisscross rhinestone trim over a red-satin finish. You know what I mean; real hooker shoes, and expensive, too.

"Oh, very kinky," goes the fat one. "I'll have a pair of them for the wife and all. Make sure you put in a size five, darling." I'm getting a pair of Satin and so's Lee when we catch Lynette's eye again and she nods to us ever so slightly. Then we get it—the heel on Satin's perfect for doing someone an injury.

Just like that Lee smashes the skinny one right on the nose with the point of the Satin stiletto heel. At the same time I go for the one with the lead pipe, and while I'm hitting him with my Satin stiletto, Lynette's twisting his wrist and making him drop the bit of pipe. Then the three of us are out the side door and into the market before the two guys got time to realize what's hit them.

There's Lynette screaming at the fruit-stall men

who are packing up their stand for the day to come and save us. The fruit-stall and flower-stall guys go into the side door of the shop like the mob and drag the two thieves out. The little one's nose is bleeding from where Lee hit him.

In the evening paper it's written up as brave-market-traders-rescue-shoe-shop-girls-from-vicious-thugs. Lee and me was really angry, but Lynette thinks it's funny. "Don't matter, girls," she goes. "We've got to let them look good sometimes. Most guys can only just tie their own shoelaces. You two going to start sorting them cartons or not?"

She's all right really, even if she does get on your nerves and everything.

Twelve Hours—
Narrative and Perspectives

by Adèle Geras

3:30 P.M. Friday afternoon. Early July.

She locked the front door behind her and walked to the corner of Marlowe Avenue, trying very hard to look as though she were merely slipping out to the shops. You never knew who might be watching. She'd said so to Alex, and told him to wait for her around the corner.

As soon as she was in the car, as soon as the door was shut, Alex's arms were around her. He was kissing her. She was breathless, laughing, trembling.

"Not here, Alex," she said. "Someone could see. . . ."

"So what? I love you. I want you. . . . I'm going

53

to shout it out of this window. . . ." He began to wind it down.

"Stop it, Alex. I haven't breathed a word to Beth."

"She must have guessed. I'm practically a fixture in your house."

"Well, she knows you're a friend, of course she does, but . . ." Linda hesitated. ". . . She doesn't know the full extent."

"Don't be so sure," Alex said, and began to drive away. "These teenagers know all about it. Every detail. Innocence is a thing of the past, I'm told."

"But I'm her mother," Linda said, sighing. "You can imagine all kinds of things, but that's impossible. . . . Can you imagine *your* mother . . . ?"

Alex wrinkled his nose.

"The mind boggles."

"Exactly."

When Beth was born, she lay in a Lucite crib: You could look through and see her tiny hands like pink sea creatures, waving above the baby blanket. I lay in bed and stared at her for hours. It wasn't only love washing over me; it was a kind of terror. I thought then: This is what "always and forever" means. Every single thing she does from now until the moment of my death will be of the utmost importance to me. And it is. The most important thing.

• • •

4:00 P.M.

Beth Taylor rang the front doorbell. There was no answer. Wearily she lifted the school bag off her shoulder and rooted around in one of the pockets for the back-door key and walked around and let herself in. This was not an unusual occurrence. Linda worked as a secretary in a school nearby, and never knew if the principal was going to drop in at three thirty and tell her to type out a riveting letter about the spread of lice among the second graders. Also, she sometimes had to shop on the way home. There was a note on the kitchen table.

> *Dear Beth,*
> *There's a meeting after school today, and then Alex and I are going to a movie and dinner. Sorry about this, but it only came up at lunchtime. Help yourself out of the freezer for your supper and do phone Pam or Rosie or Jean to visit you, but no orgiastic teenage parties, please!*
> > *See you later,*
> > *Love,*
> > *Mum*

Beth swore under her breath, screwed up the note, and threw it into a corner. Then she telephoned Pam.

"Come over after you've had supper," she said. "I'm all on my own. My mum's out gallivanting again."

"Right," said Pam. "See you about seven thirty."

Before the divorce, she was always there. That was the main thing about her: her constant presence. There always used to be a smell about the kitchen of cooking. Cakes and ratatouille mixed in with her smell, like old roses. I know, I know, said the poor distraught child, turning her tear-stained face away from the TV cameras, a Broken Home. How sad, how awful, how will I ever grow up to be anything other than a delinquent? . . . But it wasn't like that. It was what they call a "civilized divorce." Everyone is still friends . . . or says they are. I still see my dad. . . . Nothing's really changed, because I never saw him much anyway. He was always away/abroad/busy, and now he's all those things still, only not in this house. The divorce didn't make much difference to me, but it changed Mum. She got a job and she got a freezer and now bloody Alex, who's practically my age. Alex is okay, I suppose. She could have told me a bit earlier, though. Prepared me. That's the trouble with grown-ups. No consideration for anyone else. Selfish.

◆ ◆ ◆

5:00 P.M.

"Last time I played hooky, I was twelve," Linda said.

"What did you tell them?"

"That I was sick . . . that I'd be back okay on Monday."

"And do you feel guilty?"

"Guilty as hell, but not on their account."

Alex turned to look at her and raised an eyebrow.

She said: "It's Beth. . . . How do you think she'd feel if she knew her mother'd been making love half the afternoon? It's naughty."

"But nice. Like cream cakes. Come here."

Linda moved into the curve of Alex's arm and closed her eyes.

After Clive left, I thought I'd never feel anything again. Then Alex came to the school, and the very first time I saw him, I grew soft all over. For ages I just looked at him whenever I got the chance and wanted him like mad. I was like a kid, stupid and tongue-tied, rushing down certain corridors, going home down certain streets in the hope of bumping into him. I couldn't believe, still can hardly believe, that he felt what he said he felt. The first time he kissed me, behind the door of the stationery room (what a cliché!), I blushed and nearly fainted, like a young girl, weak under his hands. Now when I'm with him, it's like being drunk: It's heat and light and I have no control over myself. I'm not behaving in a grown-up fashion. He's ten years younger than I am. His skin is smooth like a small child's. When I'm with him, he's all I can think about. I've tried to be discreet at school, but I feel like an Irish Spring commercial—glowing all over, all the time.

7:45 P.M.

"I think," said Pam, "that he's pretty cute, from what I've seen."

"He's all right, I suppose," said Beth, "if you like the doomed-poet type: all floppy blond hair and long fingers."

"I wouldn't say no."

"I would," said Beth. "I think there's altogether too much sex around. I don't reckon it's good for you."

"Rubbish. Who said so?"

"I've read all about it." Beth held up her hand and ticked the points off, one by one. "First off, you can get pregnant. Then, if you go on the Pill, your hormones get screwed up; then you can get herpes and AIDS and stuff like that; and then they say you can get cancer of the cervix from it. Seems a bit bloody hazardous to me."

"When you're in love," Pam said, "you don't think about all that. You get carried away."

"I call that," Beth said, "irresponsible. She's my mum. She's got no right to get carried away. . . . She's got me to think of, hasn't she?"

"But she isn't fifteen, is she? All those things you mentioned are only supposed to happen to people our age, not to mums. Probably grown-up propaganda to keep us from having fun."

"I don't know about fun so much. . . . It sounds a bit messy and revolting to me."

"It's all different when you're in love," Pam said firmly.

"But how on earth are you meant to know when you *are* in love?" Beth sighed.

Pam pondered this question for a moment. "You know you're in love," she said finally, "when all that stuff *doesn't* seem messy and revolting anymore." She looked at her watch. "Isn't it time for that movie on TV?"

She's changed; there's no doubt about that. Her clothes are different. Well, before she only ever stood about the house and did housework, or dug in the garden, so jeans and a baggy old sweater were okay.

Now she has to have decent clothes for school; I understand that, but I don't just mean her clothes. . . . She's had her ears pierced and wears long earrings that catch the light, and she's changed her perfume. It's not soft pink roses anymore. It's a brown, smooth, thick smell, like fur. Perhaps Alex gave it to her. She wears blusher. I caught her putting on her makeup the other day. . . . Her bra was pink and lacy, and her bosom seemed to be slipping out over the top. Her panties were like tiny little lace-trimmed shorts. . . . I asked her about them and she said they were new and did I like them, but she was blushing like crazy, all the way down her neck, and she dressed very quickly after that. . . . That was when I began to suspect about Alex. There's a couple writhing around on TV this very minute. If I think of Alex and Mum doing that, I feel quite ill. I wonder if Pam really likes this movie. . . . I wouldn't mind turning over to another channel.

2:30 A.M.

Linda leaped out of bed.

"Alex! Alex, wake up, for heaven's sake! Look at the time. . . . It'll be morning at this rate before I get home. Come on, Alex, please, wake up! Beth'll be worried frantic. . . . Please."

Alex yawned and stretched and smiled.

"Relax. It's okay. I'm awake now. I'll be ready in two shakes of a lamb's tail. And don't worry about Beth. She's a big girl. She'll have gone to sleep hours ago."

"Please hurry, Alex." Linda sighed. "I knew we shouldn't have come back here for coffee after dinner. I knew at the time it was a mistake."

"No, you didn't. You couldn't wait. Go on, admit it. . . ."

"I admit it, I admit it. Now for the last time, will you get your bloody shoes on and let's get out of here!"

I wish he could drive faster. I wish we could be home sooner. Oh, please let Beth be okay. Let her not be worried. Let the house not have burned to the ground, let there not be a mad axman on the loose. Please, please don't let me be punished. I know I shouldn't have gone back for coffee, but please let it be all right and I'll never do it again. It's just that every second since she was born I've thought about every one of my actions in relation to her. Will Beth be okay? Want to go to the hairdresser? Then fix someone to pick her up from school. Want to go to the movies? Find a baby-sitter. Beth twenty minutes late back from school? All kinds of horrors flying behind the eyes. Now that she's a little older, nearly a grown-up, I feel as though I'm able to do certain things without looking over my shoulder to make sure she's all right. But not everything. Please, Beth, be all right. Don't be angry. Please understand.

3:30 A.M.

"Mum, is that you?"

"Shh. Yes, it's me. Are you okay?" Whispering.

"You don't need to whisper. I'm not asleep."

Linda came into Beth's room and sat on the bed. "Haven't you been asleep at all?"

"Oh, yes, on and off. In between worrying myself sick about you. . . . Where the hell have you been? It's bloody half past three in the morning."

"Oh, Bethy, my love, I'm so sorry. I was having such a good time. . . . I just forgot about the time. . . . I'm really sorry. I won't do it again, I promise."

"I thought you might have had a car crash. . . . You could have called, couldn't you, when you knew you'd be late. Couldn't you? And what are you giggling about?"

Linda had started to laugh, and now, weak from lack of sleep and relief that Beth was there, just the same under her flower-printed sheets, her laughter grew and grew until the tears were streaming down her cheeks.

"You should hear yourself. . . . You sound like a mother, you do honestly, and me . . . I feel like a juvenile delinquent."

"Delinquent . . . yes. Juvenile . . . I'm not quite so sure. . . ." Beth, happy to have her mother home again, even wearing new perfume, began to laugh as well.

It's like one of those books where someone wakes up one day and she's turned into someone else. Or when a family discovers their child is really a mouse or something. There's a famous one where a guy wakes up and finds he's become this huge cockroach-type creature. . . . You can see someone's point of view much better from another perspective. I always used to get real irritated when I'd come home late and see Mum peering down the road, all white-faced and frowny, but I know how she feels now. She wasn't at the movies till 3:30. She must be sleeping with Alex. That'll take some getting used to. I must get used to it. I will.

India

by Ravi Randhawa

Inderjit is the name. *In-der-jit* if you're English. *Intherjeet* with the double *e*'s dragged out if you're Punjabi. *India* if you're a friend.

We were having our first fight. He wanted to pay for our meal, but I said no, that I should pay because he paid last time. He said he never had been able to stand those Indian scenes where everyone insisted on paying for everyone else and argued for hours before paying the bill. "We should do what the English do and just pay for ourselves," he said. I said that's right, so I'll pay this time.

"Women don't pay," he replied.

"Well, this one wants to."

"This one soft in the head," his hand ever so gently brushing my hair away from my eyes.

64

"It should be fifty-fifty," I insisted. "You shouldn't pay all the time."

"I only do it because I know I'll make a profit on it," and the look in his eyes made mine look away and tighten every muscle in my body to stop the red blush spreading over my face. Oh, God! He'll think I'm really naive. What was the saying—". . . be as bold as brass." "I think everything should be shared," I said, looking him dead center, straight in the eye. "If I pay for this, you can pay for the video." His grin spread all over his face.

We were going out together. At last! If you could call meeting in the back part of a café, walking "together" on opposite sides of a street, pretending great surprise when we happened to be at the same place at the same time, "going out." We'd say wasn't it a small world and for the benefit of anyone eavesdropping we'd talk as though we hadn't met for years and years and exchange all sorts of news and ask after all sorts of people we'd never met, giving them names like "Gangrene-ganges-wallah," "Nose-picker-nosy-parker," "Nina-never-been-kissed." Stupid and childish? Yes, it was, but it was a crazy time, a Technicolor time, a shifting from black-and-white to color TV time, from living in whispers to talking out loud time. I'd read about how love makes people think they're walking on air, sing about stars and sunshine, and go around with perpetual Cheshire cat smiles on their faces. Goofy, I used to think. Off their rockers and crazy too.

I wouldn't say I'm like in love, wouldn't use that word, don't care for it. Feels like it's been through all the secondhand shops in town; you never know whose grubby hands have touched it. Even if I can't bring myself to say the word out loud, I think I've got all the symptoms. Goldfinger said it to me, but I know he'd said it to all his other girlfriends too.

"You're different, Injun." My heart used to go all soft and gooey when he called me that. "I didn't feel like this for the others."

Would you believe me if I said I believed him?

I'd had my eye on Goldfinger ever since last year, when he'd had a big thing with Christine Chambers, who sat two desks away from me. Christine was a cliché come alive: white, tall, and beautiful, with long blond hair. The opposite of me, you might say, if you were inclined to be that unkind.

"Thick as a post," my friend Suman used to say to console me. Didn't help. Christine had Goldfinger; I didn't.

I don't know when he first got called Goldfinger,

but it was on account of the amount of gold he wore; rings on practically every finger, chains around his neck, a gold watch, and it was said even his cigarette lighter was gold. Those who didn't like him, like Suman, called him Fort Knoxious. Hurt me whenever I heard it. His dad was the richest Indian guy in town, owning shops and property all over the place. My dad said you couldn't trust someone like that; they couldn't have made all that money by being honest. "Why didn't you go to private school?" I asked him once.

"You don't pay for something you can get free. How do you think my old man made his dough?"

Christine caught me looking at him once, and smiled a horrible pitying smile. After that she started taking a really friendly interest in me: dragging me along with them, talking to me about Indian families, inviting me out with them.

"Why're you always with that gruesome two-some?" Suman asked.

"I'm tagged on for effect. You know, like you don't know what's beautiful until you know what's ugly. Right?"

"You're an idiot. You're a manic obsessive. Why don't you try a white boy? Boys are all the same. If you've had one, white or black, you've had them all." Suman had done all her experimentation last year and was now a self-declared cynic. "Super Cynic Suman. That's me," she'd announced. I'd pretended to know what it meant. Wasted one whole recess searching under *s* in the dictionary.

I didn't agree with her. I didn't see how boys could be all the same. And it wasn't as if I had a choice. I didn't think I could ever love anyone except Goldfinger. Sounds fatalistic doesn't it? Like Karma and all that. My mum would really scoff at me if she could hear my thoughts; she says you've got to work for everything in life; things don't come from out of nowhere on a silver *thali*. Okay. So how was I going to get him to stop loving Christine?

Let's be honest, I said to my mirror that night, turning my face sideways, up and down, around as far as I could. Eyes, nose, mouth, teeth, cheeks, chin, ears, and neck. All the right things in their right places. Put them together and add them up and the total is—wait for it, folks . . . you're not going to believe this . . . the total is indisputably—Plain Jane India! Why didn't they total up to Beauty, like Christine's? We do our jobs, they said, we're functional, we'll help you eat, talk, breathe, look, and sleep. What more do you want? I don't want you sticking out like the Rock of Gibraltar, I said to my nose, trying to push it back, so the skin wrinkled like folds on a mountain, or these colonies of blackheads, I said, leaning forward and scratching at them. Suman had offered to squeeze them once, and if she hadn't been my best friend for years and years, I would have suspected her motives in mentioning them out loud in public like she did, just as we were lining up for lunch.

I held my breath, sucking in my "well rounded" stomach, and folding up the excess skin at the sides with my hands, I walked around on tiptoe, feeling tall, curvaceous, and glamorous. By the time I'd circled back to the mirror, my breath had seeped out, my hands had loosened their hold, and my stomach was back resting on its folds and my heels were on the floor, bringing me back to my short square shape. The mirror doesn't lie, and I said I'd be honest.

At the Christmas Dance, Goldfinger was with Precious, her black fingers intermingling with his, and I asked Christine what had happened. "He's into multiculturalism." She looked at me with another one of her awful pitying smiles: Hang-around-long-enough-and-he-may-even-get-around-to-you.

He did, too.

Suman doesn't agree, but I reckon it was going to India that did it. Mum got a letter from her parents saying that her younger brother was getting married.

She read it and reread it, and tears started running all over her face, and as she wiped them away with her *chuni,* she saw me looking at her. "Don't you ever get married and go away," she said, "thousands of miles away, not to see your parents, brothers, and sisters for years and years." She grabbed for her *chuni* again. "Use these, Mum." I shoved the box of tissues in front of her. I know she would have liked me to go around and hug her and comfort her. But I wasn't like that. I was India, born in England, ice running through my bones.

She did it when we were eating—that is, my dad and I were eating and she was standing at the stove making the *rotis.* Dad had tried to Englishize her and get her to make everything beforehand so's we could all eat together. Mum wouldn't have it. Said she couldn't have us eating stale food, only cooked us one meal a day, and that was going to be hot and fresh. *Slap, slap* went her hands, the circular piece of dough growing between her palms, then a *thump* as yet another *roti* hit the *tava.* Sometimes I'd just want to sit and watch her, fascinated by her hands moving in a repeated rhythm, going through all the different movements in making *rotis.* "I think I should go to India for Jeeta's wedding next month," she said as she placed a hot, crispy *roti* onto Dad's plate, and continued before the strangled sounds in his throat could become words. "He's the last one to be married, and it's important that one of us should be there." Her hands and eyes busy rolling out the dough. "More importantly, it'll be Intherjeet's last chance to see a family wedding before her turn comes." If Dad was surprised, I tell you, I was well and truly stunned. Didn't know what to take her up on first: missing school, taking me for granted, planning my marriage. . . . I was so astounded!

Things happened so quickly, I don't think I found my tongue till the plane touched down on Delhi airport's sizzling tarmac. I never knew sunshine could be this hot!

I couldn't move, thought my *dupatta* (classier word for *chuni*) had caught in the door. It hadn't. It was caught in Goldfinger's hands. I swear he had even more rings on his fingers than before.

"Hello, India." My heart melted so soft, you wouldn't know I had one. "You've changed."

"No, not really." Trying desperately to play it cool and wondering if Precious was with him.

"What's with all this Indian stuff?"

"Oh, well," hoping the wobble in my tongue wouldn't come through, "I'm just India returned, you see."

"I see," and there was a gap because I could see that he didn't really, so I blundered on. "It's like foreign returned! That's what people in India call people just returned from abroad."

"Why don't we go and have a coffee and you can tell me more about it." This was a chat-up line, a let's-get-together line, and this time it was for me, for real. Of course I said yes.

I did tell Goldfinger all about my trip, my words tumbling over each other in my eagerness to share with him the excitement of finding a huge, new, ready-made family, of seeing the places my parents had always talked about, of seeing things being done in the real Indian way: like shopping, for instance. It was great. You sit in front of a huge cloth-covered platform while they throw rolls of material whizzing across it and it all unfolds and flows like a river of color in front of you. I was getting all poetical when he said, "Shall we go and watch a movie on my VCR? We can get an Indian one if you want. That way we can see a bit more of India, can't we, Injun?"

I was speechless. It was like being in a movie when they're all chasing each other and everything starts going faster and faster, speeding up till you think they're all going to crash into one another, when suddenly they all stop, everything freezes. That's how I felt. Frozen. Cut off in mid-sentence.

Did things always move so quickly?

Thump, thump, said my heart. Wake up, he's asking you again. "What about the latest Amitabh Bachan?"

"What about another coffee?" I suggested, stalling for time.

"I've got coffee at home."

"I like the coffee here." I didn't want to go to his place; it was all too soon, but I didn't want to drive him away. I didn't know how I could say yes and no at the same time. "Anyway, I've got to go home soon." It was going all wrong, and here I was making it worse. "A right little good little Indian girl, aren't you," he said. Little goody two-shoes, I thought. Yes, sir, that's me. Step over the line? Not me! Won't even go near it. I didn't reply, concentrating on holding on to my tears, waiting for him to get up and leave.

"Want a sandwich with your coffee?" he asked.

I looked up. This can't be the same scene? He grinned his gorgeous grin and said, "Okay, Injun?" before he went off to the counter, and I thought, It's happening, it's really happening, and then the big horrible shapes of Auntie Bibi and Auntie Poonum came looming into my thoughts, and I knew I'd have to be careful, plan my defenses right from the start, make sure I had my alibis all worked out. I would want to tell my parents myself, when I was good and ready, but I could just imagine how they would react to hearing from Auntie Poonum or Auntie Bibi that they'd seen me with a boyfriend, doing all sorts of things that girls like me weren't supposed to: "Hand in hand, Sister. In broad daylight." Auntie Poonum always thought things were worse when done in broad daylight. "In front of the whole world, Sister. Shameless!" Knowing her, she'd stir it even more and hint that I'd been seen with every guy in town, ". . . with these very eyes, Sister," opening them both wide for emphasis.

Love. Infatuation. Schoolgirl crush. Call it whatever you want, but it really does do these funny things to you: Everything's bright and sparkling, and the dullest things become tolerable; life takes on an excitement it never had before, and with each day there's something to look forward to. Mum couldn't believe it when I gave her a huge, big, squeezy hug one day, and she wanted to know what I was celebrating. I talked to Goldfinger like I'd never talked to anyone else, not even Suman. I felt I belonged with him. If our bodies were getting to know each other, then how could our minds remain separate? We talked about white people, about our own Indian society, deciding on those things we liked about it and the things we hated about it. We played Indian music and watched Indian films, and he said, "It's such a relief not having to be a cultural interpreter," and I said, teasing a little, "What's that in English?" and instead of giving me a sensible answer like any sensible person would, he started throwing all the cushions at me, but I tickled him into submission and extracted my reply: "Having to explain every *pappadom* you eat. Now, if you don't let me go . . ." I made a strategic retreat but still got drowned in the cushions that came hurtling after me.

I felt whole and contented. All the different parts of me, the jagged ends that never seemed to fit, the bits that were English, the bits that were Indian, the bits that were just plain me, melted and fused together.

"I'm not going to have a dowry when I get married," I said one day.

"Me neither." He was laughing at me.

I wanted to tell my parents about him, to share him with them. Then, I thought, everything will be perfect. It was terribly important that it should be done properly, so I was patient, waiting to pick just the right moment. As I'd grown older, Mum had tried to warn me: She'd said, Don't get yourself tangled up—our way is better—love should come after marriage—then you know it's forever; in this country everybody shops for love like shopping for a pack of cigarettes—before you know it, you've finished the pack and got yourself a lung disease, but you're hooked, so you have to run off and buy another one. I didn't really understand all that. I wanted to say to her that when everyone else around you is trying out different brands, you can't not breathe it in too. I had giggles when I thought of introducing Goldfinger to her as my personal pack of cigarettes and saying, as I turned him around, "Look, he's so safe, he doesn't need a government health warning."

Suman and I were laughing as we came out of Ms. Missing-Something's class. Actually she was Ms. Turnbull; you know the type: jeans, holey sweaters, skinhead hair, and woman earrings. "Needs to remind herself," I'd whispered to Suman and we'd both giggled ourselves silly. She was Missing-Something because she used Ms. and not Miss or Mrs. The boys had shouted it out to her when she first came. I thought it was unfair, but she was one of those "traditional" feminists, always wearing the uniform of

the white feminist; she turned me right off. She held
a discussion and debate class for us Young Women.
We'd sit around in a circle (so trendy), clutching our
cups of instant coffee, and talk about "relevant issues." This time the talking had started off with social conditioning and moved on to the different roles
of men and women; I can't remember who first introduced the words "oppression" and "liberation"
into the discussion; frankly my mind was somewhere
else (with Goldfinger), and I wasn't really paying
attention. I sure woke up though when "Dolly Parton" Donna started going on about Indian and Pakistani women. (She really did say "Pakistani" and
not "Paki." Donna was a "friend," you see.) She
gabbled on about how they were more oppressed
than white women, kept locked up in their houses,
shunted off into arranged marriages, having to sleep
with men they'd never met before . . .

"White women do it all the time," I said, inter-
rupting her. "Never heard of a one-night stand?"

"Who'd stand Parton for one whole night?"
Suman put in, and we were the only two grinning in
the stony silence.

"Everybody knows Indian women aren't as free
as us." Parton was prepared to stand her ground;
you had to give her that. "I only want to help."

"What makes you think we want your help?"

"Because I care for women. I only want Indian women to enjoy the things we do."

"Oh, yeah," and I counted them off on my fingers. "Herpes . . . VD . . . cervical cancer . . . AIDS . . ." I could see Ms. Missing-Something looking awfully worried, her feminist and antiracist badges jiggling on her shoulders.

"How many Indian women can choose their own husbands? You tell me that, and if they haven't got a dowry, they can't get married at all."

"It's like bribing someone to marry you," said another brave spirit coming to Dolly Parton's aid.

"White women can't get married without they open their legs first." Good old Suman. Ms. Missing-Something stepped in and took over. She was upset, though she tried to hide it. She didn't tell us off; we were all supposed to be free to express our opinions; so free that she made sure none of us could open our mouths for the rest of the session, spieling on generally about cultural diversity, respect for others' customs, equal rights, sisterhood, and so on.

I guess it was poetic justice that Dolly Parton should inform me of the happy event. Came up to me after the class and asked if I'd received an invitation to

Goldfinger's engagement party. I was a bit bewildered, thinking, He's got nerve sending out invites for an engagement party without even having asked me if I wanted to; I'd imagined I'd make him get down on his knees and ask me the right and proper way. B-l-o-o-d-y h-e-l-l! That really is taking someone for granted. Parton was rummaging in her bag. "My dad does lots of business with his dad," she was saying, "so they always invite us to their dos. Here it is." She brought out a real expensive-looking card. Covered in gold, it was. Naturally. "The girl's coming from India. Some millionaire's daughter. Fabulously rich. Did you know about it?"

"Course I did."

I'd talked to him once about why he hadn't gone out with an Indian girl before, and he'd said they were hard work. They wanted to be dutiful daughters in front of their parents, but behind their backs they wanted to run around and do the same as everyone else. It's not our fault, I tried to explain. We love our parents, but we can't cut ourselves off from other people either. And we take all the risks; the boys don't. He didn't agree; he thought the girls should choose one way or the other. I talked about the parents and said how they were afraid to let their daughters go out because they felt boyfriends couldn't be trusted, a guy can turn around and do the dirty on a girl anytime he wants to. He shook his head. "Indian girls want to have their cake and eat it too."

"I think they're special; they're risk takers. Fighters. Anyway," I asked, "is that what you think of me?"

"You? You're my Injun warrior," pulling me toward him. Corny maybe, but ever so tingling-in-my-bones kind of thing.

My mind is saying something, saying it over and over again, saying to him all the time, saying: "You want to have your cake and eat it too, too, *too*."

"Why do you Indians always end your names with *jit*?" The way it was said, it could have been *git* or *shit*. He was shifting around behind me, sliding from one foot to another, shoulders twitching all over the place, hands and fingers moving on an invisible instrument. I turned back to my locker to finish putting away my books. "It's a boy's name, isn't it?" He'd shifted around to the side, the little stone in his earring winking at me.

"W-i-c-k-e-d! An Indianologist. My lucky day." I closed the door, turned the key, and bent down to pick up my bag, almost head-banging into his yellow hair as he contorted toward me, his spiky eyelashes centimeters from tangling with mine. I gave him a look that should have blasted him through the wall.

"Why've you got a boy's name?"

"Unisex." Hiking my bag onto my shoulders, I made for the door. He was a kangaroo now, jumping from one spot to another, following me.

"Since when did you guys get into the twentieth century?" he asked.

"Since about six hundred years ago." I was at the door now and was trying to get through and close it all at the same time so's he wouldn't be able to follow me. Of course it swung back and nearly hit him in the face. Remember, I reminded myself, never say sorry.

"Meow, meow." Nails scratching at my neck. Slipping my bag to my hand, I swung it around, putting my whole weight behind it. I couldn't bear to be touched; it was like he'd pulled a light switch and lit up all the things I'd been trying to hide. My bag sliced through the empty air, and he was laughing, leaning against the wall, hands in his pockets.

"One day I'll let you hit me," he said.

"Wouldn't want to contaminate myself."

"Heavy doors, those. Could do someone a real injury." He was walking beside me, human walk.

"I'm working on it."

"Lovable bit of sunshine, aren't you. What's with all this Indian stuff?" he asked, lifting my *dupatta* and letting it slip through his fingers. I tore the *dupatta* away from him, but suddenly I couldn't move, those words again, like glue on my brain. "Just stepped off the boat, have we?"

I turned and walked on, and suddenly he was a dog, yapping around my heels, making pitiful barking sounds.

"Sorry."

"People are always saying sorry."

"Sorry?"

"Doesn't change a rotten thing."

He drew his breath back in horror. "Wash your mouth out! Detergent. Bleach. Ivory Liquid—softens the toughest tongue. I didn't mean that, you know," his face wrinkling for forgiveness like a dog that knows it's done wrong. "Just a joke."

"You talking about yourself?"

"Actually," straightening up and looking human, "I'm terribly interested in Indian culture."

I sighed. Should have seen it coming. "Well, I ain't."

"Then what you wearing those clothes for?"

"Listen, you reincarnated missionary. This isn't the tropics, you know. Can't run around naked in subfreezing temperatures."

"Did you get them in Bombay or Delhi?"

My God! A man of the world. I was overcome with admiration. "Got them down at the market—goin' cheap."

"Like you?" Looked so pleased with himself.

"Missionary turned flesh trader. Figures."

"Only in female flesh," and immediately did his kangaroo jump, way back, backward. "Only another joke. Didn't mean it." Eyes on my bag, hip-hopping out of range.

This time last year I would have walloped him one for saying that. Being older and wiser, I thought, "He speaks truth who speaks in jest." (No, I didn't make it up—came from one of my Eng. Lit. books.) And now he's going to say sorry.

"Sorry. Hope you're not hopping mad about it. See you around," hopping out of sight around the corner.

"Who's the boyfriend?" Suman had come up behind me.

"Clean out your contact lenses, huh. That was no boyfriend; that was an animal."

Suman shrugged her shoulders. "Same thing. Likes you?"

"Likes himself."

"Did he try the 'I'm really interested in Indian culture' line?"

"Yeah, and slipped in Bombay and Delhi like he'd lived there all his life." We collapsed into helpless giggles.

"Next time he'll talk about integration."

"Soften me up."

"Reckon he's a culture vulture? Collecting material for his dad's book on Asian girls?" That had actually happened to Suman. We laughed so hard our stomachs hurt.

"He's not even a culture vulture; he's just a filthy lecher."

"Wow! Now who's a cynic?"

Yes. I am cynical now.

Wouldn't you be?

Hermes and Aphrodight

by Susan Price

I

There was once a young girl married to a rich old man. She was beautiful, and could embroider neatly, paint a little, and play the piano rather well. Her manners were of the most refined and modest. For some six months she embroidered, painted, played, and attended the occasional ball. Then, just as she suspected she was pregnant, her husband had an argument with his steward and died of a fit.

The young widow was sorry enough to shed a few tears at the funeral, and then she settled into a life of stifling comfort, with nothing to do but what she pleased and nothing to distract her from the miseries of pregnancy.

But month by month the estate needed more money to maintain it—more than it had ever needed while her husband had lived. The widow questioned this and that, as it came to her attention—surely no increase to her tenants' rents had been necessary? Were there really so many servants to be clothed and fed? Why were the stables costing so much more this month than last?

In time it appeared that her steward had been cheating her—and clumsily too, so low an opinion had he of his mistress's intelligence. Trembling at her own, unaccustomed anger, she dismissed him.

Now she had to manage her own affairs or risk being deceived by another steward.

She sat down at her husband's desk, opened the account books—and never had she felt so scared and helpless in her life.

All the arithmetic she knew was to count to a hundred. Ask her: What is fifty-five minus forty-five? and she didn't know, nor could she guess. The pages and pages of numbers—numbers representing terrifying, important money—dumbfounded her.

What had her education taught her of agriculture? Of the profits and losses to be made in the market? Of the maintenance of buildings? Of what use were refined manners and modesty when orders had to be given?

With much effort and humiliation, she learned some of what her husband had learned in childhood.

"What a useless thing I have been!" was a phrase that ran constantly through her head.

When her child was born, it was a daughter, whom she named, in the British way, Aphrodight. Lying in her bed, the widow thought hard about her own upbringing and the upbringing she had planned to give her daughter.

At last she said, "When Aphrodight is a woman, she will know how to manage all that is hers."

The baby was tended by a nurse while the widow struggled to master account books and husbandry, and when the baby had grown to a toddler, the words she heard most often from her mother were "Go away and look after yourself. I'm busy."

The child did look after herself, and wasn't killed by falling into rosebushes, into ponds, and from high walls, though she was both bruised and scarred. The company of her mother was a special treat, not to be expected every day, and in the time they did spend together, Aphrodight learned to read and write.

By the time Aphrodight needed tutors, her mother was a woman of some education herself, and also a woman of strong opinions and determination. She engaged tutors of mathematics and the sciences, and drew up for them an arduous timetable. They were to instruct her daughter to the limit of her understanding, and to their surprise they found the little girl both quick and eager to learn everything they could teach.

When anxious relatives said to the widow, "What of embroidery and housekeeping; what of literature and painting?" the widow replied, "These things are capable of being mastered by any intelligent person who wishes to learn them. Maths and science are practical things and must be taught, or nothing else can be done."

"But what will poor Aphrodight do for relaxation?" they asked, imagining the poor, overworked child soothing nerves frayed by chemistry in neatly hemming a long seam.

After consideration, the widow decided that they were right, and for Aphrodight's relaxation arranged lessons in riding, archery, and fencing.

As a punishment for doing badly at her lessons, she was made to learn to sew, and discovered all she wished to know about boredom by stitching long hems. As a reward for doing well in maths, she was allowed to begin learning foreign languages.

As she grew older, the tutors of her younger years were replaced by tutors more advanced in their subjects, and from her mother she began learning the business of managing the estate. At the age of thirteen she relieved her mother of the burden of keeping the account books, and by sixteen she was taking a large part in the ordering of the estate.

With pride, her mother saw that here was a girl whose manners were not of the best, who was too outspoken to be considered modest, but who would not be bewildered, or helpless, if she woke to find herself lost in a desert on a dark night. No. Aphrodight would immediately begin to navigate by the stars.

Not long after Aphrodight's sixteenth birthday, the widow discovered herself to be fatally ill. She still hoped to see Aphrodight come of age and inherit the estates in her own right, but with the strength she had learned since her husband's death, she faced the possibility that she might not, and altered her will accordingly.

The widow died before her daughter's seventeenth birthday. She left the estate to her only daughter, but until Aphrodight came of age, she and the estate were to be under the guardianship of her uncle.

Aphrodight welcomed her uncle and aunt and took her uncle through the estate accounts, demonstrating how well she understood them. She was sure that once he saw she needed no help from him, he would take no more than a nominal interest in her affairs.

That, however, was not how her uncle understood his duties. He spent a long day with her and the accounts, during which she constantly forestalled his questions with their answers, corrected his arithmetic and explained to him things she said he did not understand, called him old-fashioned, and repeatedly interrupted him with, "I *know* all that, Uncle."

He was not an unkind man, and had Aphrodight been his own daughter, or had he known her better, he might have been proud of her. But it is hard to put by your own affairs to fly to the assistance of an orphaned damsel and then to find yourself made to shuffle your feet by her superior knowledge and blunt manner.

"This is all very well, miss," he said at the end of that day, "but you won't get yourself a husband looking like that. Take yourself off to your aunt, and beg her advice on how to pretty yourself, and let me worry about the estate."

Aphrodight, who had never been spoken to so before, had nothing to say but could only stare. Her uncle, sensing what was to come when she recovered, raised his voice and said, "Humor me by accepting that until you are of age, I am in charge here, and do as you are told without answering back, miss!"

There was no peace between them from that day. Her uncle insisted on returning to the old methods of land management. He would not listen to her arguments: He had heard them all, and he was the older and more experienced. She was a child and knew nothing. Her harebrained novelties would result in ruin.

Aphrodight appealed to lawyers and magistrates, but all she achieved was a greater enmity between herself and her uncle. She was a minor, she was told; her uncle was her guardian and she must do as he said. These judgments were delivered with pitying looks for her uncle and aunt, who must contend with such a loud-voiced, argumentative, striding, rude termagant.

Aphrodight had to watch all but a couple of her valued black-and-white cows slaughtered, and the turnips that would have fed them through the winter sold at a loss. And she was subjected to hours of lecturing and wheedling from her aunt.

"You shouldn't ride so much, Apphie; it will make your bottom big. Do you have to *dig* the garden? Cut the flowers by all means, but digging. . . . Don't you think you look a trifle silly using a bow and a sword? It is no glory to our sex to ape men, my dear. Won't you put your hair up? You'd be surprised how pretty you would look. Don't sit legs apart, dear: You're a big girl now. Even a girl as thin as you should wear a corset—we all need it! What a pity you don't put on some weight. If you stayed in the house more and were more restful, you would soon have a figure."

From dawn till dusk she wittered on.

The uncle and aunt began entertaining. Every few weeks they would give a dinner party and invite, among the guests, single men and widowers. Aphrodight saw that she was expected to marry one of these men, if one of them could be induced to take a fancy to her.

She saw that if she wearied of resisting her uncle and aunt—or actually, by some self-betrayal, came willingly to marry one of these men—then the control of her estate would pass from her to her husband. If she married a lazy man, and fought hard enough, and earned herself a reputation of a harridan, a nagging shrew, she might be allowed to go on managing it, while her husband accepted the sympathy of their neighbors.

But the estate was hers, by right of inheritance and ability, and she was not inclined to use the energy that should be spent on the estate in fighting endlessly for the right to use her talents for someone else's profit.

There were, in her mother's house, many rooms. Aphrodight went, one night, to the room where clothes were kept for servants and found herself a suit of boy's clothes. She cut her hair short and threw the clippings from the window for the wind to take. Dressed in boy's clothes, tall and thin as she was, with no mincingness about her, she looked boy enough. No one, in that age, expected a boy to be a girl in disguise.

Her mother's jewels, and as much money as she could find, she packed in a money belt, which she wore beneath her clothes. Then she left her estate to go and find another—a new estate that would be hers, and hers alone, by right of merit. Or, if you prefer—she ran away to seek her fortune.

II

When Aphrodight had been ten years old, in another country and quite unknown to her, a young woman, a soldier's wife, gave birth to a son.

The very day the boy was born, the news was brought her that his father was killed. In her misery, his mother foresaw him growing into just such another man as his father and meeting the same sudden, futile death in the cause of some ungrateful king.

As soon as she was able, the mother rose from her bed and left her lodgings. Taking the child with her and telling no one her intentions, she traveled to a distant convent, a poor, bare, isolated house of women, and took up residence with them, telling them that she was a homeless widow who needed shelter from the world for herself and her little daughter, Hermia.

A boy, the woman reasoned, cannot grow up to be a soldier if he thinks he is a girl. She had never been taught about Achilles, or perhaps she would not have acted as she did.

The nuns thought the soldier's widow an over-possessive mother, for she would allow no one else to hold her child, or to wash it or change it, or even to be present when she washed and changed it. But better a mother should be too anxious than too careless.

Hermia grew into a pretty toddler, and a fierce, hard battle between the infant and her mother was fought out among the herb beds of the convent garden, and in the kitchen, the laundry, and the sleeping cell. Hermia wanted to play by herself, to run about exploring and not stay always by her mother's side. The widow, frantic that the lie she had told might be discovered if she let the child out of her sight, harshly punished each little disobedience by beating her small daughter's legs and slapping her face.

The child was hardy, and defied her mother, but this mother could not let any defiance pass.

The nuns, though not fond of noisy, disobedient

children, were shocked to see the beatings and smacks the child suffered, the number of meals she was made to miss, the few toys that were so often withheld. Was it necessary to discipline the child so often and so strictly?

" 'Spare the rod and spoil the child,' sisters," said the widow. "She must learn to be *good*, and she will never learn if I let her do as she pleases."

And though it took a year, or two, in the end the mother's greater strength and determination defeated the child. Hermia gave up the fight and, to avoid yet another punishment in her long, dreary life of punishments, stayed close to her mother at all times. She learned to obey her mother too. To obey, and obey and obey.

That lesson learned, others began. Hermia must never shout or scream but be quiet always. She must never think too highly of herself, for that would be conceited. She must never put herself forward or draw attention to herself: People would not like it if she did. "And Hermia: No one must ever see you undressed. Do you ever see the nuns or me without clothes? No. That is because we know how to behave. Always keep yourself well covered up: Don't show even your arm or your ankle. People will think you are a nasty girl if you do."

Hermia grew into a pretty but quiet girl: timidly,

nervously quiet. The nuns approved and called her polite, well behaved, modest, good.

The whole world to Hermia was the convent and its garden. She had never seen beyond its walls, for her mother had never allowed her to climb them. She knew no one except her mother and the nuns, and them not well, for she never talked freely with them.

Life seemed peculiarly pointless to her: But she was alive, and so had to live. Secretly she was not grateful to God or her mother for giving her this life, but she obediently said that she was. She felt that God had flawed her in the making. There was a fearful nastiness about her somewhere, which she was forever being punished for and forever trying to conceal without knowing what it was.

And life became more painful and perplexing as she grew older. Her voice suddenly turned against her, and squeaked, bellowed, and croaked. "This happens to some girls," her mother told her privately, in their sleeping cell, "but it is not nice to talk about it. You would shock the sisters, and I should be annoyed. You must say little and control your voice until it finds its new tone."

A new cause of punishment added to the others. Hermia became so afraid of angering her mother with her cracked voice that she almost gave up speech, and, when she was forced to make reply, whispered.

A thicker down began to grow on Hermia's body and face, a fault that her watchful mother soon spotted. "You are unfortunate," said her mother. "This happens to some women, though usually not until later in life. You must say you are ill and stay here in our room until I can get a razor and teach you how to scrape it off. Then you must scrape your face every time the hair grows."

Shame-faced Hermia, who was afraid of sharp things like razors, whispered, "Can't I let it grow?"

With wounding disgust, her mother said, "Do you see the sisters or me with *hair* about our mouths? It is your misfortune to be hairy, and you must make little of it. People don't like to see hairy girls. It is nasty. You must get rid of it."

So Hermia, for fear of disgusting the sisters, shaved secretly, loathing her own flesh, which sprouted this growth of hairs.

III

What of Aphrodight?

A year after she left her home, there came to the court of Hermia's land a young Briton named Adonis Burroughs, who presented himself before the king.

The king looked down from his throne and saw a slender boy take a broad-brimmed hat from his short, ruffled hair as he knelt. The boy's uplifted face was wonderfully, girlishly handsome, despite a long white scar above one eyebrow. The king smiled at the boy's gravity as, speaking fluently in the language foreign to him, the boy told of his education and his desire to find service at a king's court. The king liked him, welcomed him, and promised him a post.

Many people are made such promises and have hung about courts until they were penniless and despairing. It was not so for Adonis. He was young, very handsome, and foreign, and curious people invited him to their homes. The women found him more at ease in their company than many older men, and his gallantry, as he opened doors, pushed in chairs, or picked up fallen fans, had an exaggerated, playful quality they found charming.

Men found him intelligent and outspoken, quick-witted and excellent in argument. They agreed amongst themselves that he was a frank and manly boy, and a great favorite with the ladies, eh?—though perhaps too much the gentleman for his own good, since he never seemed to go further than to kiss their hands.

His popularity brought him again and again to the attention of the king and his advisers, and a position was found for him in which he acquitted himself so well that he soon rose to higher and still higher posts.

He rose so quickly that, it seemed, people woke one day to find that the foreigner, the Briton, was now a minister, and owned a grand town house and a country estate. Few people were certain how this had come about; and many people were jealous.

Even those who had once liked Adonis began to turn against him. He is unmarried, they said, but he does not keep a mistress; or if he does, he keeps her very secret. And he is *such* a favorite with the king.

Those friends who remained faithful to Adonis gave him simple advice. Marry, they said. Find some heiress. Increase your wealth and secure your standing in our country by marrying her. There must be a dozen such girls whose fathers or guardians would gladly marry them to you.

"There are, in every country," Adonis said, but made no attempt to act on their advice. Some of his friends then wondered if the rumors were not true.

IV

What of Hermia?

Her mother died so suddenly that she left no will nor was even able to tell the nuns what arrangements she wished made for her daughter. The mother superior therefore thought it best to search the few papers left by the dead woman and to write to a man whose name and address she found in them.

This man was the brother of the dead woman, and he came quickly to take his niece away from the convent. For years he had known nothing of the whereabouts or well-being of his only sister, and now he determined to do all he could for Hermia. After all her years in the convent, he would give her as much fun as he could pay for and marry her as well as was possible.

Hermia's uncle was a minor official at the king's court and had three daughters of his own, so he was not rich; but he was a kind man, and generous within his limits.

Hermia's aunt and cousins, eager to meet her, were disconcerted. Their nun-raised cousin was a large, blockish girl, with a pretty but frightened face and a manner so constrained, awkward, and clumsy that all in her presence were affected by it, and soon found themselves as wordless and witless as she.

Hermia would rather have remained in the nunnery. Everything outside was so noisy and busy, so shocking. She was expected to share a room with her eldest cousin, and to help her cousin dress and let her cousin help her. This broke all the rules Hermia had been so thoroughly taught, and scandalized her.

Shy as she was, she was driven to protest and, when she was teased and laughed at for being so sensitive, became desperate and hysterical, until her new family were alarmed and rearranged their entire household in order that Hermia could have a bedroom to herself.

This did not endear her to her aunt or cousins, and she made matters worse by sneaking away to her room and locking herself in several times a day. When she was nagged by her aunt to make an appearance in the family's living room, she would creep in and sit hunched near the door, her head bowed and her arms hugging herself, her whole body draped in an ugly convent dress. She hardly spoke, and when she did, it was in a whisper.

"This girl will never find a husband," said her aunt. "Let her go back to the convent."

But Hermia's uncle felt he had rescued her from the convent. "Let her see a little life," he said. "Make her some pretty dresses, do her hair, and take her to a ball. She's a pretty girl, really. She'll soon blossom, you'll see."

Making a ball dress for Hermia was not easy. She didn't want to go to a ball and wept when she was laughingly assured that she would enjoy herself once she was there. She would not be measured for her dress because she said it was indecent for her to be seen half dressed even by her cousins. To arguments she remained silent and tearful, returning no answer but plainly not changing her mind. Her aunt could have slapped her. Her dress had to be made from measurements taken from one of the dreary convent dresses. And Hermia would not have it in bright colors, or even white. It must be dark blue, black, or gray. And it must have sleeves to the wrist and a neck to the throat.

"You say you don't want to stand out, but you *will* stand out in such an ugly dress!" said one of the cousins.

Hermia would not listen, and when the evening of the ball came, she was a hunching, sneaking, dowdy figure beside them in their bright colors and flounces. Standing among them, Hermia took sneaking looks at their arms, and at their breasts in their tight bodices, and was confused and frightened by how different they were from her. Had her mother lived with her in such seclusion for so many years because of how different Hermia was from other girls? Was everyone who looked at her hiding their disgust at her ugliness?

Hermia hated the ball. Every beautiful woman there made her feel more loathsome, but worse was seeing so many men with hair about their mouths and wondering again about the hair that grew on her own face, and other places. Did all people have such hair, and did only women shave it? Or ... ? But she knew she was a girl.

This ball was only the first of many. Though her aunt was furious and called her a clod who made no effort to be attractive, her uncle was convinced that soon she would grow used to her new life and become a beauty.

And then, with all the other families of all the other court officials, they attended the King's Birthday Ball; and to that ball came the king's favorite, the foreigner, the Briton, Adonis Burroughs.

Adonis was the first man Hermia had ever seen for whom she felt something like the feeling her cousins said they felt for three out of every five men they saw. Many men were called handsome, but this Adonis *was* handsome—he was beautiful. And though his movements were as swift and ungoverned as those of other men, he was so slight of build that they did not alarm. His voice was deep, but not very deep. He never raised it—people fell quiet to hear what he had to say. When he came near, people fluttered.

Hermia's uncle went up to him, on God knew what pretext. Hermia, watching, saw Adonis Burroughs look toward her aunt and herself—and the foreigner's eyes fixed themselves on her!

Frightened, she looked away—and so did not see the expression of shock cross Adonis's face. Other people saw—and heard Adonis ask to be introduced to the family of a minor official. An overwrought tale of love at first sight was later woven around this incident.

Adonis was gracious to Hermia's aunt and cousins, and bore with their giggling attempts to be the most witty, the most vivacious, the most unusual. He took Hermia's hand, kissed it, looked long at her lowered head, and said that he hoped to know her better. Turning to her uncle, he asked permission to call on him, and this permission was hurriedly granted.

"What *can* he see in her?" Hermia's aunt said to Hermia's uncle. "It must be because he's British."

Hermia could not stand their looks, smiles, nudges. What could a man so handsome and rich want with the ugly, hairy, disgusting girl that she was? She knew it all to be a huge, vicious joke: But she did not know how to end it.

V

It takes a thief to catch a thief and a trickster to catch a trickster. Alone in the ballroom, Adonis recognized Hermia. For though Hermia was a figureless, grace-less girl, what reasonable person would look at her and think her anything other than a girl? And though Adonis was a slender and a small man, who could ever believe that he was anything but what he declared himself to be?

Women are women, after all. They enjoy being girls, and their heads are full of ribbons and bows, hairstyles and marriage. What woman could hide her womanliness and be a man? Men are men. They are naturally strong and rebellious, full of old Adam and hard as nails. It is still harder to believe, for the reasonable person, that a man could ever be disguised by long skirts, necklaces, and lace, or that the spirit of Cain could ever be reduced to a womanly meekness.

But Adonis Burroughs looked at Hermia and thought: If I must marry to silence the gossips, here is a girl I could marry!

And so Adonis Burroughs, the king's foreign favorite, came to call at the house of Hermia's uncle, and he told the uncle of his wish to marry his niece.

For the next half hour Adonis had to listen to the man expressing how very flattered and honored he felt: how certain he was that Hermia would feel flattered too, how he and his wife had never expected such honor, and so on, and so on—when all he meant was, "How wonderful it will be to have someone rich in the family!"

Finally Adonis was able to ask if he might speak to Hermia alone.

"Of course, of course. Come this way, to the drawing room. Everyone else will slip out, and you can talk—of course, the drawing room isn't fit to be seen, not by such as you, but—you understand, of course."

The entrance of Adonis Burroughs, and the disappearance of all her relatives, was for Hermia the beginning of a new torment. Adonis was so handsome, she felt she had no right to be alone in a room with him, any more than an old and crumbling house brick has any right to be set side by side with a cut-glass bowl in a glass case. But to leave the room would be rude, and she could not be rude.

She could not look at him. He sat near her and explained, in his gentle, light voice, that he wanted to marry her and had her uncle's consent. At this, her head was filled with such a noise of panic that she could hardly hear or understand him. Such phrases as she did catch only renewed the frightened gabbling of her mind. Such phrases as, "I shall always keep your secrets. . . . I trust you will keep mine," and, "We must be honest with each other and wear our day-to-day disguises only for other people. . . ."

It all sounded so *intimate,* and people must never touch. Hermia set her teeth and endured until, receiving no response whatsoever, Adonis left her to herself.

Adonis took leave of his host and hostess, and returned home with a puzzle and a problem. Not only did her aunt, uncle, and cousins believe Hermia to be a girl, but Hermia believed *herself* to be a girl. Could it be that she was right? If the marriage went ahead, as Adonis had no doubt it would if he wished it, would he find himself married to a girl? That would be a wedding night more fraught than most.

Subsequent meetings, however, convinced him that Hermia—like so many other people—was not what she was dressed up to seem.

The wedding date was fixed, and Adonis bought gifts for his bride to be, whom he had not even kissed, for merely holding her hand sent her into a rigid panic, so prudish was she and so unworthy of him did she feel.

From the king's goldsmith Adonis ordered, in strictest secrecy, two small, golden figurines, to be made naked.

"That won't please her," said the goldsmith. "Nudes aren't the fashion. Most people won't have them in the house." But Adonis insisted that they be made naked and delivered secretly to him without anyone seeing them.

The wedding was held at Adonis's town house. There were hundreds of guests, quantities of food and drink, hours of music and dancing, and a long, long ceremony.

Hermia wished the tedium might crawl by more dully and slowly still. The longer it went on, the longer she could live without the cruel embarrassment and shame that must eventually follow. When midnight came, though, even she began to wish that it might end. Disaster had come to seem preferable to the agony of anticipating disaster.

Adonis rose from the table and held out his hand to her. Trumpets sounded, and Hermia's face tightened and turned white. She rose and put her hand in his. Like a wooden peg doll she tottered after him on fear-stiffened legs through ranks of their guests, who raised a tremendous noise of celebration with cheers, whistles, clapping, until Hermia's face was as burning red as it had been pale. But as soon as the newlywed couple had left the room, the guests forgot them and went back to their food and drink.

No servants waited in Adonis's room. He locked

the door, smiled, and said he had one last present to give her before they went to bed. He led her to a small table, on which stood something covered with a white cloth. Adonis pulled away the cloth and revealed to her two beautiful, naked, golden figures.

One was of Aphrodite, the other of Hermes. Their names were engraved on their plinths.

"Which is the goddess?" Adonis asked.

Obediently, Hermia pointed to the figure of Hermes in its winged sandals; but then drew back her hand and stood in confusion as she saw the god's name on the plinth. Yet she was a girl, and her body was like that of the Hermes statue.

"There is no mistake," Adonis said. "The goldsmith is a man, and made the god as he knows a man to be and the goddess as he knows a woman to be."

This was hard for Hermia to understand. She was being lied to, or had been lied to—but who was the liar? Then her husband unbuttoned his tunic and shirt and revealed breasts like those of the goddess.

Hermia was so white and overwrought that Adonis took her by the arm and led her to a chair by the fire. He sat in the opposite chair and began to talk.

Hermia listened in astonishment and admiration

as Adonis confessed to being Aphrodight and told of her upbringing, the coming of her uncle, of how she had left her home and country, and of how she had taken service with the king and had risen to his— or her—present rank.

Hermia, who had led such a closed and timid life, was thrilled to hear of such courage and to be sitting so close to one who had dared to take such risks and had outbraved them all to such good end. Whether her husband was a man or a woman, and whether she herself was male or female, Hermia fell in love with the voice, with the words, with the courage, of Aphrodight-Adonis.

The story Hermia hesitantly told in return was far less enthralling, and well she knew it. A sad story of punishments and groundless fears, of ever-increasing timidity and failing courage until, at last, she was almost afraid to move from the place where she— or he—sat. And throughout, she had been certain she was a girl.

Aphrodight listened with pity and, at the end, looked out of the window and saw that day had come. She rose, called servants, and ordered a carriage. Returning to her bride, she said, "Today, now, we shall go into the country. No one will know you there, and Hermia shall become Hermes."

And by the evening of the next day, Adonis Burroughs and his new wife were at their country estate, far from the capital.

VI

In time, Aphrodight's estate was rewon, and they went to live there. Needing no rest, Aphrodight set to work and made the world inside her estate boundaries a good one. Sometimes she wore a man's clothes, sometimes a woman's. The clothes made no difference to her, for they hid only some details of her body; and people who met her could not say, a moment after, what her clothes had been. The body, the person, within the clothes remained the same, whatever their style. Aphrodight and Adonis were the same person.

But Hermes never put on a woman's clothes again; and he changed so that, even though his face remained the same, he could never have been recognized. From crouching and whispering, he sprang straight and shouted. Revolted by his own helpless ignorance, he turned to Aphrodight and learned from her all he could. Through their common cause in giving and taking, learning and teaching, their attachment to each other became so strong, it was unshakable and would have been trivialized by the name of love.

Their affection and loyalty were made incarnate by four children, all daughters, the eldest of whom inherited the estate.

The other three were all remarkable women, of talent and energy: And all four of them were proud to boast that their mother had been a great statesman, and their father almost a nun.

The Year of
the Green Pudding

by Fay Weldon

The personnel department? This way? Thanks.

Sir, you have a nice face. I reckon I can talk to you.
Tell you about myself? Why not! That's what you're
there for, after all.

It must be possible to live on this earth without doing
anyone any damage. It must be. I try to be good. I
really try. I rescue wasps from glasses of cider; I look
where I'm going so I don't tread on ants. The second-
worst sound I ever heard was when I went to rescue
a lamb tangled up in an electric fence, and there was
a crackle underfoot and I was treading on snails,
cracking their shells, piercing them, killing them.
Why did so many snails congregate in one spot?

113

There was no reason I could see, except mass suicide. But no excuses for me, I should have looked where I was going: The lamb could have waited a second longer; the snails would have been saved. The second-worst thing I ever did was murder a duckling. Not on purpose, of course, but definitely murder by neglect. No excuses. I went to put the ducks away for the night, to save them from the fox. I heard a *cheep, cheep,* and assumed it came from inside the shed. I should have checked. I didn't. The sound came from *under* the shed. I was deaf to the *cheep, cheep, cheep,* the little plea for help as darkness fell and the bright eyes of predators gathered in the hedge. I wanted to get back into the warm for a cup of coffee. In the morning there was no duckling. I reckon the rat took it, that blond little, silly little, helpless thing. I saw the rat later, a great fat brown hairy mean thing, and I let it go. I could have taken a stick and beaten it to death. But it had a right to live. Why should the rat's ugliness, the duckling's prettiness, condemn the rat to death? Yes, sir, I was brought up in the country.

What was the worst thing I ever heard? It was the sound of Cynthia's crying outside her bedroom door, where I lay inside with her husband. Crocus we called him. He had a thick thatch of yellow hair, which brightened up dull rooms. Cynthia was my best friend, so you understand the "we." The worst thing I ever did? Why, to be there with him in the bed.

I'm a middling sort of person, don't you think, sir? Of middle height and middle size, and I buy the kind of clothes that are labeled S, M, or L: kind of floppy, not tailored. I choose the M. My hair, left to its own devices, is mid-brown, and my shoes are size five, the middle size, they say, though I think statistically sixes are more normal now. Our research department says the population's getting bigger. My eyes are a kind of middle gray, and I wear a medium makeup base. Really, I'm sometimes surprised people recognize me in the street. I smile a lot, as you'll have noticed, showing these middling-even teeth, but my friends sometimes complain I have no sense of humor. I just think they're sometimes not very funny in what they say and do. For instance, I think Irish jokes are dangerous and cruel, and I also think one has to say so, out loud, there and then, if anyone begins. There's one joke I heard recently that did make me laugh, out loud. It goes like this. "Question: How many radical feminists does it take to change a light bulb? Answer: That's not funny." So I do have a sense of humor. Anyway, that's enough about me.

· · ·

Why am I here? My department head sent me to discuss my resignation. Did I mention that I'm a vegetarian? No? Actually, I try to be a vegan (that's someone who doesn't eat any dairy foods, never mind just the cow itself, both on health grounds and because if eating the cow is murder, drinking the milk is theft), but I don't always succeed. I'm like A. A. Milne's king—"I do like a little bit of butter on my bread." I hope all this doesn't make me sound rigid and boring; I don't honestly believe I am. I just do try to get by doing as little damage as I can. And I make a very good onion-and-potato pie!

That's since Crocus. Not the pie—not doing damage. What happened about Crocus is this. I was twenty-five. A funny sort of age: not really young, but not really old; just too old to enter the best beauty contests. I felt more on the shelf then than I have done before or since; I don't know why. Cynthia, as I say, was my best friend. She and Crocus had a little boy of two, Matthew. They'd had to get married because Matthew was on the way. Cynthia wasn't much good with babies, and I was around there a lot helping. I wasn't married, I had no children, I was just more competent than she was. It wasn't difficult. She once put salt in his bottle instead of sugar. She shouldn't have put sugar in anyway: It's unnecessary and fattens without nourishing, but try and tell Cynthia anything like that. Cynthia wasn't middling to look at, not at all. Cynthia was narrow waisted and long legged and long backed and had natural blond hair, one of those white, fragile skins that go with it, and dark blue eyes, the blue you see when you look out of the Concorde's window. (I have been on the Concorde: I am full of surprises. Crocus used to say I was full of surprises.) I talk of Crocus in the past tense because it's all over between him and me, and Cynthia's in the past tense because she's all over. She's dead. What happened was this. I know I'm a long time getting around to it, I'm sorry, it's just so dreadful, I rattle on and put it off.

Concorde? I was working on the liver pâté account. They were serving it on the Concorde, on little pieces of toast with the free champagne cocktails. The client offered me a free flight. Why are you so interested in the Concorde?

Cynthia went to the hospital to have her second baby. She'd had a dreadful pregnancy, poor thing; the baby was pressing on the sciatic nerve. I moved in to look after little Matthew—and Crocus. Cook meals—you know how men are not supposed to be able to.

Though if you ask me, they just don't want it known quite how good they are, in case it gets around. She was in for forty-eight hours. I think Crocus and me could have got through that even though we were alone. I mean talking formally and not catching each other's eye, though what he wanted was to be in bed with me and what I wanted was to be in bed with him, and we both knew it. Not saying, not touching, made it stronger; that's the way it goes. The whole air crackled between us. But we could have held out; I know we could. Cynthia would have come back and it would all just have faded away. Things do. But the hospital called and said the baby wasn't up to its birth weight: Cynthia wouldn't be back till Saturday. That was the Wednesday. And on Wednesday night, after visiting hour—he'd taken chocolates (Crocus was like Cynthia: He never would believe just how bad sugar is for you) and I'd taken grapes—we came straight back and went to bed together. Not the spare room—it was too near Matthew's room—but their bed, Crocus and Cynthia's bed. I told you about his hair, didn't I? Blond! Cynthia had dark-red pillow slips. I shall never forget—and Thursday evening we went to see her again, at visiting time, with never a flicker, all that sex didn't seem any of her business, somehow, and the new baby was just lovely, and Matthew seemed really fond of it—it was a girl—and Cynthia said she wanted to call her after me because I was such a good friend, and do you know, I felt not a twinge of guilt. Does that make me odd, or just like anyone else? I didn't mean to hurt her, but Crocus and me—it just seemed more important than anything else: What made the world go around and the stars shine and the wind blow and so forth. And all of Friday, when Matthew was at play group, and as soon as he'd been put down at six o'clock, we were in the bedroom—actually, not in the bed, most of the time, on the floor—does that make it better or worse? And then suddenly the door opened and there was Cynthia and the baby. She'd discharged herself, we later heard: I don't think because she suspected anything; she just didn't like hospital food—not enough sugar, I suppose—and knew the baby was doing fine in spite of what the hospital said.

She shut the door quickly so she couldn't see us—it took us some time to get ourselves together, or rather not together—and we could hear her weeping the other side of the door. Just quietly weeping.

Crocus went out to her, but she didn't stay; she just handed him the baby and left. And by the time I'd got myself together—I never was a fast dresser—and he'd handed the baby to me and gone after her, it was too late. She went down the subway and threw herself under a train. The poor driver. I think of the poor drivers when anything like that happens.

Anyway, that was that, sir. Crocus couldn't bear to be in the same room with me afterward, and I think I'd have screamed if he'd touched me. It just sort of shook us right out of it. The young one didn't get called after me, that's all I know. And that she'd been on antidepressants and had threatened suicide in the past. Neither of them had told me that. So what sort of friendship was it? Do you think they were ashamed or something? Shouldn't you be frank, with friends?

But that was the end of my love life, at least for a time. It put me right off men, I can tell you. I got the blame, of course, and it ought to have been forty percent of the blame—fifty percent each and an extra ten percent for him because he betrayed a marriage partner, which is worse than betraying a friend. But of course I got a hundred percent of the blame from all and sundry, especially men. I moved out of the district and I got a job here. I'd always wanted to work in an advertising agency. But now I have to resign. Why? I'll tell you.

• • •

I do believe if you try, sir, if you really try, you can get through life without causing damage. I just hadn't been trying over the Cynthia-Crocus business. I did, after that, I promise you. I checked up on all my dates; if they said they were married, I wouldn't go out with them; I wouldn't even be alone with them. If they said they weren't married, or divorced, I still checked up on them. Thirty percent who said they weren't, were, can you imagine that? And the other seventy percent—I just wasn't interested. I was working as a secretary then, sir, not a copywriter, as I am now, but hoping, always hoping! Yes, I do get to meet the clients. I suppose I am attractive, in my middling kind of way. You know how it is—there'd be business lunches, business dinners: But I'd just go off home, I was so discouraged, frightened of trouble. I think that client who sent me off on the Concorde got really cross, but I couldn't help that. If you don't feel anything, you don't feel anything. And then I met Martin. You know Martin; he's an art-group head here. Attractive? Crocus was nothing to Martin. You know how it is; you touch and there's this surge of electricity—it's almost as if you've been stung? And I thought to myself, Look, I can't go on atoning forever for what I did to Cynthia and her children, if I did, because that's what I've been doing. I've got to have children of my own, get married, settled, somehow, sometime. And Martin was crazy about me. And I was crazy about him. And I thought this is really working, really something—you know that kind of confidence you get when everything's in balance?

And then he told me he was married. I hadn't checked up, I didn't want to check up, I didn't want to know. But he told me. He said theirs was an open marriage, she didn't mind. I minded. I said no, that's it, that's the end. He said go and visit her: And I said no. What would she do if I visited her? Walk straight around under the nearest train?

"No," I said. "Never."

He brought her around to me. She said I was welcome to him. She'd met somebody else: She wanted a divorce. I was to feel free, to make her feel better.

So I felt free. By God, I felt free. At last, it seemed to me, a penance that I thought was endless had worked itself out. I was free to be happy. The anxiety lifted. I hadn't realized what it was, this black, terrible cloud I'd been living under. Anxiety. If you've suffered from it, you'll know what it's like; if you haven't, sir, count your blessings. It's like a physical pain, only it's attached to your feelings, and there's no cure for it because it has no reality, no real cause in the outside world, so you're free to attach it to any number of things. But what are you anxious *about*? they ask. The answer you give is air crashes, or AIDS, or you've forgotten to turn the gas off, or you've offended your best friend (that's always a good one for me), but the answer is not *about* anything; it's just anxiety, free-floating anxiety, and you'd rather be dead but you're too anxious about failing to try. I guess Cynthia wasn't anxious. Just depressed. But Martin cured me of every sad, negative feeling I ever had. It's been a wonderful year, a whole year of happiness. We became proper vegans together; we jogged, being careful not to step on snails; we joined the League Against Cruel Sports, until we decided it was cruel to humans; and I taught Martin not to kill wasps but just to sit still and leave them alone and they'll leave you alone, and to pick spiders out of the bath with a postcard and cup. Then you lot gave me a promotion at work. I actually became a copywriter! It seemed to me I could love Martin and do nobody any harm.

But now it's January second, and I have to hand in my notice to you, sir. I have to, sir. This is what happened. Haven't you heard? You know I'm on the fresh-ginger account, sir? And that we took all those full-page spreads in the women's magazines? And that I did the recipe for the Christmas pudding? And that it went in in July, so that everyone's puddings would have time to mature by Christmas? I didn't check the recipe, sir. I was too happy with Martin to bother. I remember thinking, Shall I check this through once again or shall I quickly, quickly go downstairs to the cafeteria and meet him for a drink? You get somehow starved of some people, at a certain stage in a relationship, and really suffer if you can't see and touch and be with them. And that was the stage Martin and I were at. And I didn't check the recipe. I forgot to put the sugar in. The typist left that line out and I didn't check. And, sir, those full-page spreads are read by tens of millions, and one in ten actually made the pudding, covered it with foil, left it to mature, put it in boiling water on Christmas morning, turned it out piping hot after the turkey, and it was green. Green. Mold. Inedible. Green puddings by the million, sir, and my fault. A million Christmases spoiled, because I was in love.

Yes, I said "was." Every bit of feeling's vanished. I don't think I could bear to touch Martin now. I don't know what it was all about, all that feeling, all that kissing, all that love. Except I seemed doomed to cause trouble. I'm never going to fall in love again, sir, never, never, never.

Sir, there is a little brown spider by your elbow. Don't move, you might squash it.

The Contributors

Sandra Chick
Sandra Chick's powerful first novel, *Push Me, Pull Me*, dealing with sexual abuse in the family, won the 1987 Other Award. Ms. Chick lives in Bath, England.

Adèle Geras
Adèle Geras lives in Manchester, England. Her feminism comes across in the range of female characters she includes in her work and in the themes she tackles, for example in *The Green Behind the Glass* and *Voyage*.

Jean MacGibbon
Jean MacGibbon's autobiography of her early life, *I Meant to Marry Him,* was published recently to great critical acclaim. "The Sexy Airs of Summer" she dedicates to her granddaughter, Hannah MacGibbon, who helped her write it.

Susan Price

Susan Price lives in Dudley, England, and has written many novels and short stories for young readers, from *Sticks and Stones*, set in a supermarket (after she had worked in one), to *Twopence a Tub,* the story of the Dudley coal miners' first strike.

Ravi Randhawa

"India" is Ravi Randhawa's first published work. She is a young Indian woman living in London, and she coordinates the Asian Women Writers' Workshop.

Jacqueline Roy

"A Family Likeness" is based on Jacqueline Roy's own family history—her father was the celebrated Jamaican sculptor Namba Roy. Ms. Roy's first novel, *Soul Daddy,* was published in *Teentracks* magazine.

Rosemary Stones

Rosemary Stones has reviewed children's books for *Spare Rib* for ten years. She has written a study of sex-role presentation in children's books, *Pour Out the Cocoa, Janet,* and has recently compiled a bibliography of nonsexist children's books for Penguin, *Ms Muffet Fights Back.*

Fay Weldon
With such novels as *Female Friends, Down Among the Women,* and *Remember Me,* Fay Weldon is well established as one of Britain's foremost feminist novelists.